Everything was gone.

Except for the flattened area where their tarp had stood, there was no sign that a camp had ever been there.

Delia cursed as she realized that whoever had taken their things had taken her canvas duster and her hat. She looked around in vain for anything that he might have left but found only a scrap of plastic from the groundsheet. The sleeping bags, ropes, stakes, their packs, their hiking boots — everything was gone. All they had left were the clothes on their back and the survival kit Delia carried around her waist. There was only enough food for a few meals, and the snow would make hunting difficult. She planned on building a travois when she retrieved Beth from the ledge; pulling it would require plenty of calories. She worried about the man and whether he would return.

It began to spit snow. There was no time to waste thinking about the obstacles she faced in getting Beth off the ledge. She had to act now.

About the Author

Jeane Harris lives in Arkansas with her son and a cat, Socrates, whose rear end is now as big as a Buick. She is an Associate Professor of English.

DELIA IRONFOOT

BY JEANE HARRIS

The Naiad Press, Inc.
1992

Printed in the United States of America on acid-free paper
First Edition

Edited by Katherine V. Forrest
Cover design by Pat Tong and Bonnie Liss
    (Phoenix Graphics)
Typeset by Sandi Stancil

Library of Congress Cataloging-in-Publication Data

Harris, Jeane, 1948–
    Delia Ironfoot / by Jeane Harris.
        p.   cm.
    ISBN 1-56280-014-0
    I. Title.
PS3558.A6463D4   1992
813'.54--dc20   91-38869
                                                                          CIP

This book is for Mary Sue
who gave us safe harbor in Utah
and for Lisa
who gave me my life back.

Acknowledgements

The author would like to thank the following people for their love and encouragement during the writing of this novel:

Jill Lively, my "island rising," Tree, Stick and Scouffie who love their Swami, "Hammer" Adams who listens patiently, Eric who took the pictures, Schof, a son with whom I am well pleased, Wild Nick Tours, Robin who always gives me a place to stay, my gradual students at ASU who have kept me humble, and the Columbia Cubs who keep me young.

Chapter One

Delia Ironfoot pulled the tractor alongside the entrance to her uncle's barn and turned off the engine. She jumped down from her seat atop the John Deere and pushed back the white baseball cap with the leather bill from her forehead. Looking out over the field at the neat bales of alfalfa, she pulled a bandanna from the back pocket of her khaki pants and wiped her face. Tomorrow she and her Uncle Robert would load the hay and stack it in the barn; if they were lucky her twin cousins, Will and Tawny, would be around to help them. Over the weekend she would load up her share to take back to her ranch at Half Moon Lake.

She stuffed the damp bandanna into her pocket and squinted up at the sun. It was the first week of September; in an hour or so the sun would sink behind the jagged peaks of the Uinta Mountains that even now cast long shadows across the alfalfa field. She inhaled deeply, enjoying the sweet-acrid mixture of earth, hay and diesel fumes. She loved this time of evening when the work was done, and she could actually look back at what she had accomplished. Maybe it wasn't as exciting as traipsing all over the world trying to prove an archaeological theory that no one else believed — especially her colleagues at the university — but it was much more peaceful and safe.

A mental image of herself sitting in a doorway staring out into a trash strewn street flashed into Delia's mind and like a chain reaction other painful memories followed — the humiliation she had felt at being denied tenure, Robin's betrayal, her father's death — all the memories that she had tried so hard to put behind her.

She looked around for Neji and spotted the enormous dog lying just inside the entrance to the barn. Delia called to her. "Come on, girl. Time to go."

The hair along Neji's broad back stood up but not in response to Delia's call. Rising to her feet, Neji lumbered toward the road that ran along the west side of the field. Delia squinted into the setting sun and saw her Uncle Robert's battered red pickup truck bouncing along the dirt road. Neji bounded alongside the truck inside the fence until it pulled into the long driveway that led up to the house and barn. As Robert climbed out, he bent down and briefly scratched the stiff hair along Neji's back before walking over to Delia.

A tall, broad-shouldered man with deep-set black eyes and long straight hair pulled back into a braid that reached halfway down his back, Robert's broad, flat features were expressionless without being unfriendly. He wore a wide-brimmed cowboy hat, faded jeans and a denim work shirt. His ample waist was encircled by a beautifully tooled leather belt with a Navajo-made silver and turquoise buckle. To Delia's mind, he looked at the world around him with great interest, and his most endearing characteristic was his idiosyncratic expressions that only people who knew him well could understand. Looking out over the neatly mown rows of alfalfa, he nodded.

"Not bad for a ditch digger." He paused. "Or a college professor."

Delia took off her cap again and ran her hand through her short salt and pepper hair. Robert always referred to her former profession as "ditch digging" or, in more serious moments, as "grave robbing." Even though Robert was only half-Navajo, he viewed death like most Navajos — as a final, terrible evil. There was no transcendence to a higher plane, no happier level of spiritual existence. Death brought ghosts and ghosts could bring sickness to an otherwise healthy person. Robert's mother's blood flowed through his veins and the idea that someone, especially his own niece, would dig up dead bones repulsed and frightened him.

"Uncle, I'm not a college professor or an

archaeologist anymore. "I'm —" Delia paused and looked around her at the fields and the mountains. "I'm here."

Robert's face never changed expression, but when he spoke again his voice was full of disgust. "They were stupid people. They didn't understand what you were trying to do."

Delia sighed inwardly. Her Uncle Robert and his wife Lilah still blamed her colleagues at the university for her breakdown, and although Delia had tried to explain to him many times that it had resulted from more than just seeing her career in ruins, they didn't understand. None of her relatives did.

"No, Uncle. That's the problem. They understood perfectly." She stopped. She didn't intend to have that conversation again. It brought back the most painful year of her life.

She asked, "Did you get a chance to talk to the twins and see if they can give us a hand tomorrow?"

Robert turned to face her and nodded. "Yeah, I saw them. They're eating dinner at the jailbird's, soaking up some of his air conditioning."

Delia silently translated this particular piece of information. The "jailbird" was Nephi Wixsteader, a convicted tax-evader and Mormon polygamist who owned the only gas station and air conditioned restaurant in Bittercreek. At seventy-five, he still worked behind the counter of his restaurant and could often be seen filling gas tanks at the pumps outside.

"Did they say they'd help load hay tomorrow?" Delia asked.

"They can't," Robert said. "They've got a track

meet at BYU tomorrow. Guess it's just you and me."
He eyed Delia. "Is that okay?"

"Of course it's okay," Delia said. "Why wouldn't it
be okay?"

Robert shook his head. "I just thought since you
had a client down at the jailbird's you might be too
busy tomorrow to help."

Delia looked at him with surprise. "Client? What
are you talking about? I don't have a group
scheduled for three weeks."

"Well, there's a woman down at the jailbird's
asking questions about you."

"What kind of questions?"

"Asking if anybody knows how to get hold of
you."

"Hmm, that's weird." Delia frowned. "Maybe she
got my name from that book."

Robert might have been smiling though it was
hard to tell. "You mean the one for women only?"

Delia looked at him sharply. Robert never openly
referred to her lesbianism, though her preference for
women had never seemed to bother him the way it
did some of her other relatives. The Navajos
generally had no problems with lesbianism, but the
Utes considered it a perversion. Robert had spent
most of his life with his mother on the Navajo
reservation in Mexican Hat in the southeastern
corner of Utah and in this case at least, his Navajo
nature, and his love for his niece, outweighed
whatever reservations he may have had.

"Yes," Delia told him. "I wrote those people and
told them I don't do raft trips anymore." She looked
at her uncle defensively. "It's true. I don't."

Robert said nothing which was fine with Delia.

She appreciated silence which was why she felt comfortable with Robert and with her uneventful life at Half Moon Lake. Which was now threatening to be interrupted by a total stranger. She winced inwardly remembering the last group of women she had taken on a raft trip. City-weary, rich lesbians who knew nothing about the outdoors and who had to be reminded every day to pick up their trash and were disgusted when she told them they would have to pack out their own body wastes.

She leaned against her truck. She wanted to drive home, put her feet up on the porch railing and drink a beer. All day, while she baled hay in the hot sun, she had relished the idea of the porch and the beer. But instead of looking forward to an evening of quiet watching the moon come up over the lake, she would have to go into Bittercreek and hunt around Wixsteader's until she found the woman who was searching for her by name.

Delia turned back to her uncle. "Did she say how she found out about me?"

"Nope," Robert replied. "I didn't talk to her. I just heard her asking around."

"Great," Delia muttered, slipping into her long canvas duster. She turned down the corduroy collar and called to Neji. "Well, I better go find out what she wants." She touched her uncle on the shoulder. "I'll be back tomorrow."

Robert followed her to her truck and watched as Neji leaped in beside her. "You know the worst part?"

Delia sighed. "No, what's the worst part?"

"It's late and she doesn't have a place to stay."

"Well, she'll just have to drive over to Harrison

and find a motel," Delia said firmly. "I have to get home and take care of my animals." She paused. "Shawla went to Salt Lake to see her sister."

Robert shook his head at the mention of Shawla, but he did not pursue the topic. "Harrison's got that Dinosaur Days Rodeo this weekend. There won't be a hotel room anywhere. She'll probably have to drive back to Salt Lake to find a room."

Delia started the engine and buckled her seat belt. "Then that's just what she'll have to do because I'm not taking her home with me, and I'm sure not taking her on a raft trip."

Robert Ironfoot watched his niece drive off down the dirt road. When her truck finally disappeared around the bend he shook his head and started toward his house where he knew his wife was preparing supper. He smiled as he thought of Delia's vow not to take the woman home with her. Ordinarily when his niece stated her intention to either do or not do something, he believed her. She was a willful woman, like her mother and her grandmother. They were all willful. His grandmother had been willful to marry a Ute, and his sister Rose, Delia's mother, had married a white man from the South. Sometimes Robert thought it would have been better for everyone, especially Delia, if their ancestors had stuck to their own tribes. They would have had less trouble in their lives. But the trouble had made them all strong, and Delia's time of trouble had demonstrated to him that she had inherited her family's strength.

It still pained him to think of the thin, hollow-eyed woman he had found in Denver on that cold November afternoon over four years ago. At first he thought she was drunk, she was so unresponsive. When he found out that she wasn't drunk, indeed had never been drunk in her whole year of wandering, the knowledge frightened him. Some other sickness had afflicted her soul. He had put her in his truck and driven directly to Mexican Hat where his mother, Delia's grandmother, had accepted the woman that the family had seen only a few times before. His mother, Ruth Many Sheep, was convinced that Delia was bewitched. She had convinced her friend (and sometimes lover) Bernard Hasjohn to say a Blessing Way for Delia.

Robert smiled at the memory. Hasjohn hadn't wanted to sing for a white woman; Robert suspected that part of his reluctance also had to do with the fact that many of the people in Mexican Hat still had hard feelings that Ruth Many Sheep, a highly respected woman in her clan, had married a Ute. It helped some that she had finally left her husband and come back home. She wasn't the first Navajo woman to be charmed by a Ute cowboy at the Four Corners rodeo. Delia's grandmother had explained to Hasjohn that Delia was at least part Navajo and therefore deserving of the ritual. Robert didn't know if it was the Blessing Way that had restored Delia to mental health or simply time. But he was happy that after she recovered, she had moved to Utah.

As he entered the house and smelled the dinner Lilah had prepared, he thought that it would be interesting to see whether Delia stuck by her intention not to take the woman home with her once she actually met her.

Chapter Two

Wixsteader's was almost empty when Delia arrived. The evening was getting late, at least by Bittercreek's standards, and even customers who had lingered over a last cup of coffee had gone home. Like her and her Uncle Robert they had hay to mow, bale or load the next day. With Neji at her side, Delia waved to Yolanda who was wiping the counter and straightening the napkin dispensers and menus. Yolanda looked up and Delia pointed down at Neji questioningly. Yolanda nodded and waved her assent. Delia looked down at the dog and said,

"Stay, Neji." The dog lay down obediently by the cigarette machine and put her massive head down on her paws. Her eyes followed Delia as she moved away, but she didn't budge from her spot. She would stay there, motionless, until Delia returned.

Delia acknowledged a few greetings from some of the men and women sitting in the booths along the wall. Her eyes scanned the restaurant and quickly found the woman who had been asking questions about her. She didn't fit in with the sunburned ranchers and farmers who were finishing up the last of the meatloaf special.

After pausing at the counter to get a cup of decaf from Yolanda, Delia walked over to the blonde woman sitting in the last booth in the back of the restaurant. The woman looked up at Delia's approach and as she drew nearer, Delia saw that she was older than she first thought. Thirty-five instead of twenty-five, Delia decided. Her ash blonde hair was fashionably cut and styled. Well-tailored slacks and a dark blue polo shirt contrasted starkly with the faded jeans and work clothes of the people around her. The woman wore white-soled boat moccasins and a gold Oyster Rolex. Delia noted gold earrings and a necklace that looked as expensive as the watch. The only discordant aspect of her pampered appearance was her deeply tanned face and forearms. It wasn't the kind of tan one got from working in the yard on weekends or from a sunbed.

A half-filled coffee cup and the *Wall Street Journal* were at her elbow with an aluminum briefcase, a cellular phone nestled inside, open on the table in front of her. Next to the phone lay an old issue of *Ms.* magazine; a younger Delia Ironfoot in a long yellow canvas duster with a small pickax in her hand smiled up at her from the cover. The headline on the magazine jumped up at her: "TRACKING DOWN OUR HERSTORY IN AFRICA WITH DELIA IRONFOOT — A WOMAN'S ANSWER TO INDIANA JONES."

The woman's eyes went to the magazine and back to Delia's face. "Well, I'll be damned," she said with a flat midwestern accent. "It is you."

Delia moved toward the booth, determined to get the meeting over with as soon as possible. The woman stood up and hastily moved her windbreaker from the seat. "Sit down. Please."

Delia removed her duster and folded it on her lap. She sat quietly looking at the woman, trying to decide what she wanted. Until she had seen the copy of *Ms.* she thought the woman was probably just another bored, rich lesbian wanting a week in the wilderness. Now she thought it might be something different. As she tried to decide, a soft burring sound emerged from inside the briefcase. The blonde woman said, "Hold on a sec," and picked up the phone.

While she waited for the woman to get off the phone, Delia wondered if this might be another university offer. Since her own prestigious Ivy League school had denied her application for tenure five years ago, other universities from time to time had contacted her with teaching offers. Sometimes journalists doing "Where are they now?" stories found her, though the last one must have spread the word to her colleagues that there was no point in going all the way to Utah since Delia had refused to even speak to her over the phone. But this attractive woman did not look like a university provost with a teaching offer and though she did have the intense look of a journalist, her intensity seemed to spring from a different source. Judging from her clothes, hair, jewelry and briefcase, Delia thought the intensity probably had to do with making money. Lots of money.

"I'm not sure when I'll be home, Jack," the woman said. "Maybe a week or two. Well, Utah *is* in the continental United States. Uh-huh. Just watch gold prices and don't wimp out on the oil. I'll call you in the morning after the exchange opens. Don't sweat it. I'm gonna hold your hand, Jack. Yeah, me too. Talk to you later."

After she replaced the phone, the woman turned to Delia. She seemed to have gotten over her surprise.

"Sorry for the interruption. I'm Beth Collins — I'm from Chicago. I heard about you from ... well, of course, lots of people have heard about you. But I personally heard about you from some friends you took on a raft trip about three years ago." She paused. "I wrote you a letter a couple months ago but I never got an answer."

She stopped and sipped her coffee, as if waiting for Delia to speak. When Delia remained silent, she went ahead. "I'm a stockbroker — under a lot of pressure at work and I needed to take some time off. I remembered my friends telling me about you and I thought a trip would be just the thing to —"

"I'm sorry," Delia interrupted. "I don't take people on raft trips anymore. It's too bad you came all this way but ..." Delia stood up and began putting on her duster. "It was nice meeting you, but I have to go home."

Beth Collins squinted up at her in disbelief. She seemed rooted to her seat until Delia actually walked away. Then she jumped up and grabbed Delia's arm. Delia turned and found herself looking into a pair of blue eyes fringed with thick dark lashes, a startling contrast to the ash blonde hair. She realized how beautiful Beth Collins was. Standing this close to her, she could smell her shampoo and soap, and just a subtle hint of perfume. Delia could also see tiny wrinkles around the corners of her very blue, intense eyes and a sunburned patch of skin on her nose.

Delia sensed that because Beth was obviously well-off, she was also probably used to getting her own way, which accounted for her stubborn hold on Delia's arm. A hold, Delia had to admit, that was not totally unwelcome. Against her wishes, she felt a momentary spark of warmth in response. It was her turn to be surprised and ... disturbed. Since Robin ... She pushed Robin from her mind, as she always did, and moved away from Beth slightly.

"Hey, don't go off half-cocked," Beth said, drawing Delia back into the booth. "I'm not interested in river rafting. I want to go backpacking. Look, I really need to talk to you. Just hear me out."

Delia reluctantly lowered herself back into the booth with a sigh. "I don't take individual people backpacking. I take groups of people llama trekking. Anyway, I wasn't kidding about having to go home. I need to feed my animals."

"Llamas? Aren't they kind of like camels?"

"No, not really."

"Well, don't they sort of look like camels?"

Delia stared at her without speaking. Beth held her gaze and once again Delia felt the force of her personality.

"So," Beth said. "Not that it matters, but why don't you take people on raft trips anymore?"

Delia felt a surge of annoyance at the woman's prying questions. "It's a long story," she said.

"Okay," Beth said briskly. "Do you really speak eight languages?"

Delia smiled in spite of her annoyance. "Why?"

Beth grinned. "I'm curious. Do you?"

"Yes."

"You really speak *Turkish*?"

"Flawlessly."

"No shit. Say something in Turkish for me."

"Look," Delia said, her patience exhausted. "I really don't have time for this."

"You know, when my friends first told me that they had gone on a raft trip in Utah with Delia Ironfoot, I didn't believe them. I mean I'd read about you in *Ms.* and *National Geographic* but ..." Beth looked down at the magazine in her briefcase. "I've always been kind of interested in archaeology. That was pretty shitty what happened with your teaching job at ..."

"Are you a reporter?" Delia interrupted her. "Because if you are I *really* have nothing to say to you." She started to get up, and once again Beth put out a hand to restrain her.

"Hey, hold on," she said, frowning. "I'm no reporter. I told you, I'm a stockbroker."

"And you want me to take you — just you — on

14

a backpack trip. And you came all the way from Chicago on the off-chance I'd be free?" Delia looked at Beth intently. Beth's glance didn't waver the way most people's did when they lied; nevertheless, Delia knew she wasn't telling the truth. She wondered why she would lie about something like backpacking.

Against her will, Delia was intrigued. Not only with Beth and the way the laugh lines around her eyes crinkled when she smiled, but with why someone would travel all the way to Utah and then lie about why she had come. There had to be more to the story than Beth was telling. And Delia was still curious about Beth's outdoor complexion that seemed at odds with her indoor occupation.

Delia finished the now cold cup of coffee and started to button up her coat. "I can't take you," she said firmly. "And now I'm really going. I have a long way to drive."

"So, what kind of animals do you have?" Beth asked.

Although it was obvious to Delia that Beth was stalling again, she admired her persistence. And she did seem interested. Delia felt her attitude soften a little. Anyone who was interested in animals couldn't be all bad. "Two dogs," she told her. "One is over by the front door."

"No kidding?" Beth craned her head to look. "Jesus, he's a monster. What kind of dog is it?"

"African Ridgeback," Delia told her.

"What's its name?"

"It's a female," Delia informed her.

"Okay. What's the female's name?"

"Neji."

"No shit? What kind of name is that?"

"It's African — in Liberian folktales Nejis are water nymphs."

"Imagine," Beth murmured. "Where did you get her?"

Delia felt a twinge of pain that she associated with Robin and she shook her head. "Another long story."

"Okay. Where's the other one?"

"The other what?" Delia was having a hard time keeping up with Beth's questions. In some ways the questions annoyed her, but, on the other hand, she didn't feel quite as much urgency as before to leave.

"The other dog. You said you had two."

"Oh," Delia said. "I have an old dachshund. Sam. He never leaves the ranch."

"What else have you got?" Beth asked.

"Look, as fascinating as talking about myself is, I'm exhausted and I can't take you and I am going home. Now." Delia stood up and put her cap on with the bill facing backwards. Beth's shoulders slumped forward, and she too appeared exhausted.

"Where are you staying tonight?" she reluctantly asked Beth.

"Damned if I know," Beth admitted. She pushed her hair back and suddenly she looked younger and more vulnerable. "I flew in early this morning and rented a car in Salt Lake City. Then the waitress here told me there are no hotels in this godforsaken place. She tells me the nearest hotel is in a town that's having some rodeo or hoedown — I called over there. Guess what? No vacancies." She looked up at Delia. "Look, how much do you charge to take people llama trekking for a week?"

Delia shook her head. "Money isn't the point."

"Well, what if it was the point? How much would you charge?"

"Look — I ..."

"Come on, what do you charge when you take a group?"

"It depends on how many."

"What's the minimum number you'll take?"

"Six."

"And how much does it cost per person?"

Delia told her.

Beth whistled. "Tell you what, I'll give you twice that if you'll take me." She reached into her briefcase and pulled out a checkbook. "I'll write you a check right now."

Delia shook her head. "I don't have time. I'm helping my uncle load hay tomorrow. And it's going to be even harder now that some help we counted on can't be there. Look, I'm very tired."

Beth reached out and took Delia's hand. Her hand was surprisingly strong; even more surprising were the rough callouses Delia felt on her palm. Another mystery. How did a Chicago stockbroker get callouses?

"Tell you what. I'll help you out with the hay — load it or whatever you do with it. If you'll take me packing."

Delia looked at her with amusement. "You'll help me load hay," she said. "Have you ever loaded hay before?"

"Nope."

"Have you ever even *seen* a bale of hay?"

Beth looked insulted. "Of course I've *seen* a bale

of hay before. I live in the Midwest for God's sake. There're bales of hay all over the place."

Somehow this response struck them both as hilarious and they started to laugh. Delia suspected that it was their exhaustion that gave Beth's retort its humor.

Delia looked around the empty restaurant. She didn't feel like hassling with Beth anymore and saw no way to dismiss her without feeling guilty. She had no intention of taking her backpacking, double her usual fee or not, but she couldn't just leave her either.

"It's too late for me to drive home now anyway," Delia said wearily. "We'll just stay at my uncle's. We can sleep in the bunkhouse."

"You mean, you *will* take me?" Beth said hopefully.

"No," Delia said firmly. "You can stay at my uncle's and in return you can help us bale hay tomorrow. That's a fair trade."

She thought she heard Beth mumble something under her breath but when she turned to look at her, Beth looked innocent.

"What about your animals?" Beth asked as she gathered up her briefcase, newspaper and windbreaker.

"I've got a CB in the truck," Delia said as they walked to the register. "Somebody's bound to be up around my house."

"What about my rental car?" Beth asked, slipping into her windbreaker.

Delia took out some money to pay for their

18

coffee. Yolanda waved it away and continued to wipe the counter.

"Yolanda, this woman is leaving her rental car in the parking lot for a couple of days. Tell the sheriff not to tow it, okay?"

Yolanda nodded. "Couldn't tow it anyhow. Jake's gone to Wyoming for the weekend. No tow truck." She reached under the counter and brought out something wrapped in aluminum foil. "I set this piece of rhubarb pie out for Shawla. It's her favorite."

"I'm not going home tonight," Delia said. "I'm staying on to help Robert stack hay tomorrow. I'll tell her you thought of her though." She looked down at Neji. "Okay, girl, let's go."

The dog stood up and followed the two women outside. As Delia walked toward her truck, she heard Beth behind her speaking softly to Neji: "I saw the way you looked at that piece of pie. I know, I can't believe they didn't give it to you either."

"I wouldn't try to pet her if I were you," Delia said casually over her shoulder. "She doesn't like strangers. She might take your finger off."

Beth looked down at Neji in mock alarm and said, "You wouldn't do that, would you, girl?"

To Delia's amazement, Neji looked up at Beth with an interest she rarely showed in humans and answered her with an amiable woof and looked, if not happy, at least content to let Beth scratch behind her ears. Delia shook her head and continued walking toward the truck.

The wind had shifted to the north since the

afternoon; the air was crisp with the scent of sagebrush and a promise of fall. Beth shivered and pulled her windbreaker around her. "Damn, I should have brought a heavier coat," she muttered.

"It gets cold here at night," Delia told her.

"Ha!" Beth laughed. "Don't talk to me about cold. I'm from Chicago. I know about cold."

She opened the trunk of the rental car and took out two large leather suitcases and an overnight bag. Delia noted with mild curiosity that in addition to the suitcases, the trunk also held two cardboard boxes and a brown duffel bag.

"What do you want me to do with these?" Beth held out her suitcases.

"Leave them," Delia told her flatly. "You're not staying long enough to need them. Just bring the overnight case."

"Well don't feel obligated to let me down easy," Beth muttered as she put the suitcases back and slammed the lid. She handed Delia her overnight case, and Delia tossed it into the back of the pickup where it landed next to a roll of barbed wire, a posthole digger and a spare tire.

"Hey, take it easy with that," Beth said. "That cost two hundred dollars."

Delia looked at Beth disdainfully and motioned to Neji who jumped up into the bed of the pickup. Before opening the truck door on the driver's side, Delia straightened the old horse blanket that covered the exposed springs of the seat.

"Well, what are you waiting for?" she asked impatiently. "Get in."

Beth obeyed and gingerly settled herself on the blanket. As soon as they were on the highway, Delia picked up her CB and spoke into the receiver.

"Breaker, one-nine. This is Digger. Come on."

There was a burst of static, silence and then: "This here's Smokey Bear, Digger," a laconic male voice said. "Come on."

"Hey, Smokey. You anywhere near my place? Over."

"Not too far. Me and the Italian Stallion been on a burn over at Flat Top today. Over."

"On your way back to town could you stop at the ranch and check on the llamas? The horses can stay in the corral, but the llamas need to be put in the barn for the night. Their food's in the tack room, on the left side as you go in the barn. And you could check on Sam — make sure he's got food. Over."

"Lucky you. We ain't goin' back to town. We're campin' out near your place. Not that I mind doin' it, but where's Shawla? Over."

"She's visiting her sister over in Salt Lake this weekend. Over."

"Oh, the sister again. Okay, I gotcha. You be back tomorrow? Over."

"I think so. Over."

"Okay. We'll go by tomorrow evening too just in case. Over."

"Appreciate it. Over."

Delia replaced the CB receiver and turned off the main highway onto a bone-jarring dirt road. The truck bounced in and out of a massive pothole, causing Beth to bump her head painfully on the roof of the cab.

"Ouch, dammit! What was that all about?" Beth asked, rubbing her head. "Who's Smokey?"

"Smokey's my friend, Nick Andretti. He works for the Forest Service."

Delia felt Beth stiffen next to her. "Forest Service? You mean from the office here in town?"

"No," Delia said, looking over at her. "He works out of the District Office over in Harrison. Why?"

"No reason," Beth said nonchalantly. She cleared her throat. "How did you know he'd be near your house?"

"When I saw him and Lou last weekend, they mentioned something about a controlled burn near Flat Top. That's near my house. So I took a chance they'd be there . . . and be listening to their radio."

"Oh," Beth said. "Who's Shawla? Your lover?"

"You sure ask a lot of questions that aren't any of your business," Delia observed coldly.

"Oh, come on, loosen up. Who is she? No, let me guess — it's another long story? Right?"

"That's right."

"Are all your stories long ones?"

"They are to people I don't know," Delia said. "Why do you ask so many questions?"

Beth shrugged casually. "I'm a curious person." She paused. "Did I hear you mention something about a bunkhouse?"

Delia nodded.

"A real bunkhouse? Like — cowboy-type bunkhouse?"

Delia nodded again. "My grandfather built it a long time ago to board the extra men he hired during the cattle roundup in the fall. We always called it the bunkhouse. It's where I sleep when I stay at Robert's."

"Great," Beth muttered, as they hit another pothole and she banged her elbow on the door. "Smokey's on the CB, tonight we sleep in the bunkhouse and tomorrow I load hay."

"Welcome to Utah," Delia said.

Chapter Three

Delia's irritation at not being able to go home returned when they arrived at Robert's. As she walked into the bunkhouse, she automatically reached for the light switch and then remembered that the house had never been wired for electricity. She stepped inside.

"Ugh," Beth said from behind her. "This place stinks."

Delia ignored Beth's observation and looked around for the kerosene lamp she remembered from the last time she had stayed in the house. She found a dusty, half-filled lantern on the table and, after some difficulty, managed to light it. The lamp didn't do much to improve the atmosphere; what its sickly yellow light illuminated was not a cheerful sight. Dust covered the rough planked floor and cobwebs festooned the low ceiling.

"Oh, God!" Beth exclaimed. "It looks even worse than it smells." She put her overnight bag on the wobbly table and looked around in dismay. "I can't sleep in here."

Delia felt exhaustion and frustration sweep over her. "Would you rather drive back to Salt Lake City or sleep in your car?" She turned away from the source of her irritation and called to Neji. "Come on, girl."

"Where are you going?" Beth asked, as Delia began walking toward the door.

"I'm going to feed Neji." Delia fought to keep her voice even. "You'll find some blankets or sleeping bags in that closet over there."

Beth looked at her in disbelief. "How can you stand to sleep in this place? It's filthy."

"I've slept in a lot worse," Delia retorted, as she let the screen door slam behind her.

Delia strode angrily across the yard between the bunkhouse and her uncle's, Neji padding beside her. She opened the door to the back porch and looked around for the plastic trash can full of dog food that she knew Robert kept for Neji. Finding an empty pie tin on a shelf, she filled it with dry dog food and carried it back across the yard to the porch of the bunkhouse. She could hear Beth inside on her cellular phone talking to someone — Jack, she assumed by her shushed, outraged tone.

Neji sat down on the porch and looked up at Delia expectantly. Delia put the food down and watched Neji eat. Inside she heard Beth muttering to herself about dirt and bugs. A few minutes later Beth opened the door and swept a huge cloud of dirt in her direction.

"Sorry, Neji," Beth said, her apology apparently not extending to Delia. Delia got up and moved Neji's dish and herself to another corner of the porch. Later Beth again came to the door, this time with a bucket in her hand.

"Is there any running water around here?" she said, her earlier weariness apparently having been replaced by outrage.

Delia pointed to a pump at the end of the porch and watched as Beth pumped a bucketful of cold water and retreated into the house again. As she heard Beth pouring water into a basin, an image of Beth taking off her clothes floated unbidden into Delia's mind. Closing her eyes, she dozed fitfully, waking a short time later with the heavy, warm weight of Neji's head on her thigh.

Inside the bunkhouse was quiet, Beth's cleaning frenzy apparently over. Delia arose stiffly, massaging her bad knee, and went inside.

The light from the kerosene lamp seemed softer now, and the cabin looked considerably cleaner. Wet streaks on the floor indicated that Beth had wet the broom and swept the floor. Beth sat on the edge of a cot she had pushed against the wall, as far away from Delia's cot as she could get. Dressed in blue pajamas, Beth was brushing her hair which looked soft and golden in the lamplight. Her beauty, so unexpected and vivid against the shabbiness of the bunkhouse, stabbed Delia painfully. She felt the ache move up into her throat, but she swallowed it.

"It looks better," she said sincerely.

Walking over to her own cot, she found that Beth had shaken out a sleeping bag for her and arranged it neatly. The act of kindness made her regret her earlier irritation, and she turned to Beth to thank her, but Beth had already crawled inside her sleeping bag, her back turned to Delia.

Sometime in the night, a noise awoke Delia, and she looked through the small window beside her bed to see the moon, orange and full, hanging above the top of the cottonwood trees. The sight filled her with a sudden and unexpected loneliness and sadness she hadn't allowed herself to feel for a long time. She rolled over on the hard narrow mattress and was greeted by the golden glow of Beth Collins' hair shining in the darkness. Reaching down, she let her hand fall on the short stiff hair on Neji's back, and with the dog's reassuring bulk under her hand, she drifted back to sleep.

The next morning, before she and Beth went over to Robert's house for breakfast, Delia rolled up her sleeping bag and turned to Beth.

"You don't really have to help us load hay." She turned her attention back to her sleeping bag so that Beth couldn't see her face. "If you want, I'll take you into town and you can drive back to Salt Lake."

"Can't do that," Beth said firmly. "I told you — I need your help."

Delia turned around, puzzled. "Help? What are you talking about?"

Beth looked momentarily confused. "Nothing. I didn't mean help. You know what I meant. I need you to take me backpacking. That kind of help. Besides, you need my help with the hay." More collected now, Beth put her hands on her hips and looked cross. "You don't think I can do it, do you? You think I'm some kind of goddamn wimp."

"There's no need to curse," Delia said firmly. "It's just — well, it's not really a fair exchange. A full day of loading hay for a night in a dirty room with no electricity or running water."

Beth ran her hand through her shining hair and arched her back. "Don't forget the lumpy, hard bed with no sheets." Then she shrugged. "Forget it. Anyway, you'll see. I'm no weakling."

As they walked across the yard to Robert's house, Delia said, "I'd appreciate it if you'd try to curb your cursing in front of my aunt and uncle. They're not used to that kind of language."

She noted with satisfaction that Beth flushed with embarrassment.

When they entered the screened-in porch that was Aunt Lilah's summer kitchen, Delia's aunt was putting a second pan of buttermilk biscuits into the oven of the wood burning stove. Huge wooden shutters were propped open to let the cooling breezes from the mountains sweep through. Robert had built the kitchen thirty years ago for his beautiful Paiute bride. Over the years, he had offered many times to build his wife a regular kitchen with modern appliances that most people took for granted, but Lilah had refused.

"I like to do things the old way," she would say. All her beds had feather mattresses filled with down from her geese, and all the blankets on the bed and rugs on the floors and walls were woven with wool from Delia's llamas and from her sister-in-law's sheep which she carded and spun herself. Delia had never seen her aunt idle.

Lilah greeted the two women with a platter of steaming biscuits, her round brown face flushed with the heat from the stove. "I was so embarrassed when I woke up this morning and saw your truck in the driveway, Dee," she said.

Delia glanced across the table at Beth who arched her eyebrows and mouthed "Dee?" to Delia who ignored her.

"To think of you staying in the little house," she said, putting plates on the table. "No one has stayed in that house since ... I guess it was two months ago when the twins were here. I cleaned it then, but it gets so dusty." She looked out the screened panel and sighed. "The wind from the mountains blows and dirt comes in every crack."

Robert entered the kitchen carrying a large metal pail. "Oughta buy my milk in plastic jugs at Safeway like everybody else."

Delia's aunt turned to Delia and Beth and winked. "You have said that every morning for almost fifteen years, old man."

Robert poured the milk through a cheesecloth

into a clean jar. "Well, it's been true every morning for fifteen years."

"Uncle Robert, Aunt Lilah, this is a ... friend of mine from Chicago," Delia said. "Beth Collins — Robert and Lilah Ironfoot."

Beth nodded to both people and sat down at the oilcloth covered table. She put a dollop of preserves atop a biscuit and closed her eyes as she chewed. "This is without question the most wonderful biscuit I've ever tasted," she said sincerely.

"Thank you," Lilah said, pleased with the compliment. "Have as many as you like. I've got another pan in the oven." She turned to Delia. "Your uncle tells me that Shawla is off to Salt Lake City again."

Delia buttered her biscuit lavishly. "Yes," she said reluctantly.

"When was the last time?"

"I don't know. About six weeks or so."

"Honestly, Dee. I know you feel that Shawla saved your life but ..."

"She's fine," Delia asserted. She didn't want to talk about Shawla in front of Beth.

"She's an unhappy woman," Robert observed.

"She's fine," Delia repeated stubbornly.

As Delia and Lilah talked, a shaft of sunlight caught the golden tints in Beth's amazing hair and once again Delia was struck by her beauty.

"I guess you haven't had showers yet," Lilah said as she laid thick slabs of ham in a cast iron skillet.

"No," Delia replied as she buttered herself another biscuit. "I think I'm more hungry than dirty."

"Well, that's no way to treat your guest," Aunt

Lilah said. She motioned to Beth and they walked into the house, Lilah explaining to Beth about water temperature and towels.

"She's not my guest," Delia mumbled, joining her uncle at the kitchen counter where she washed and dried her hands. She felt his gaze upon her and looked at him.

"It just happened," Delia said defensively, drying her hands on a towel. "She offered to help us load hay if I would take her backpacking. But I said no."

"Can she load hay?" Robert asked, doubtfully. "She doesn't look very strong."

"I doubt it," Delia replied, cutting off a piece of ham that was sputtering in the skillet. "She's a stockbroker — from Chicago." She shrugged. "She didn't have any place to stay last night. This morning I offered to take her back into town. She said no."

Delia sat down at the table and put the piece of ham between the two halves of a biscuit. "She's rude. She asks personal questions."

"She wants to help us — let her help," Robert said, turning the ham slices that Lilah had left on the stove.

Lilah came into the kitchen and took the fork from Robert's hand. She cracked eggs into the skillet. "Go sit down and eat," she told Robert.

As Robert finished his ham and eggs, Beth, dressed in a pair of Delia's old Levis and a faded red cotton T-shirt, slid into her chair. Her hair was wet and her face shiny, but she still looked beautiful. Delia's jeans were too long for her and she had rolled up the legs.

"I gave her some of your spare things that you

leave here, Dee," Lilah told her. "She said you wouldn't let her bring her suitcase with her." She turned back to the stove. "What will she think of us? The little house dirty, and you won't let her bring her own clothes?"

"Don't worry about me, Mrs. Ironfoot," Beth said graciously. She smiled sweetly at Delia and began buttering biscuits. "I'm just fine. Dee," she emphasized the word, "kept apologizing for the bunkhouse but I told her I didn't think the house was bad at all." She took a bite of her biscuit.

Delia stared at her, flabbergasted by her lying, but Beth merely smiled at her.

"How do you like your eggs?" Lilah asked Beth, as she put a plate in front of Delia.

Beth looked quizzically at Delia who was tucking into a full plate of ham and fried eggs. "Uh, that's okay, really, Mrs. Ironfoot. I don't want any eggs or ham. Biscuits will be fine."

Now it was Lilah's turn to look puzzled. "Biscuits won't stay with you very long, girl. Loading hay's hard work." She turned to Delia. "I cannot believe you are making your guest work."

Delia glanced up at Lilah and then over at Beth. "She's not exactly a guest, Aunt."

"Oh, it's all right, Mrs. Ironfoot. I don't mind at all. Delia said she needed someone to help today and I was more than willing to help a friend."

Delia stared at Beth in amazement and shook her head. "I do not believe this," she said under her breath.

"Well, you can't stay here another night if you

keep calling me Mrs. Ironfoot. Call me Lilah." Lilah patted her arm before returning to the stove.

"Where are you girls headed for after we finish loading?" Robert asked innocently.

"We *girls* are not headed anywhere," Delia said firmly. She picked up her plate and looked hard at Beth. "I'm going home tomorrow night and Beth is going back to Chicago." She went to the sink, rinsed her plate and turned around. "We better hurry up. We haven't got all day." And with that, she stomped out of the house.

After three hours of loading hay, Delia knew she had underestimated Beth Collins' physical stamina and strength. The woman attacked the backbreaking job of lifting and loading the fifty pound bales with the same fervor and intensity that she had attacked the dust and dirt of the bunkhouse the night before. Even Delia, who was used to outdoor physical labor, began to slow down after three non-stop hours in the hot sun.

No one Delia had ever talked to had suggested that cutting hay was a pleasant way to make a living. The dust and particles of alfalfa got down inside clothes and inside every orifice of the body. The leather gloves that were necessary to avoid having your hands shredded on the baling string caused your hands to sweat, and eventually your fingers and palms were rubbed raw from the leather sliding back and forth across wet flesh. Then there was the sneezing and coughing as the sinuses tried to rid themselves of the irritating dirt and hay. Delia remembered Nick telling her once that even if you'd never had hay fever before, you would develop it after cutting hay for a while.

Too, rabbits and field mice made their homes in the hay, and when the mower went over their nests, the results often showed up red and bloody in the bales. Haying was definitely not a pleasant job.

As the morning stretched into early afternoon, the day turned warm. The sun began to evaporate the moisture trapped in the hay and the air became damp and humid. Delia noticed during one of their water breaks that Beth looked tired and suggested they break for lunch.

Lilah greeted them with platters full of food — pan fried steak with gravy, mashed potatoes, coleslaw, fresh corn and green beans from the garden, leftover biscuits from the morning and a pitcher of iced tea.

"You look like you could use some nourishment," Lilah said, touching Beth's shoulder as she slid down into her chair. "Iced tea?"

"Yes, please." She shook her head at Lilah's offer of sugar. "Boy, loading hay is fu—" she caught Delia's glare and said, "Fun. Hard work but, gee whiz, *really* fun."

"You have some pretty strange ideas about fun," Robert observed dryly. "Better have more than biscuits or you'll never finish the day," he advised as she helped herself to the vegetables and slaw. He speared a piece of meat and held it over her plate. "Here — have some steak. It'll give you strength."

Beth shook her head. "No, really." She looked at Lilah apologetically. "Actually, I'm a vegetarian."

"Oh," Lilah said, looking at her blankly.

Delia kept herself from smiling at Beth's announcement only with great effort. She cut her own beefsteak deliberately into thin strips and spread her biscuit lavishly with pale sweet butter.

Beth stared pointedly at Delia's biscuit which was dripping butter onto her plate. "I mean, everybody knows that saturated fats, sugar, eggs, red meat — those things can kill you. They're full of chemicals and preservatives. You never know what's in your food."

"Yes, I've heard that too," Lilah admitted with a small frown. "I guess we're luckier than most." She laughed and patted her round stomach under the apron. "We eat pretty good. I have a big garden every year and we have an orchard and some grapevines. We have our own chickens and geese. We have that crazy cow Robert bought. Everything we eat, we raise ourselves."

"No sh— I mean, really? Everything?" Beth asked in amazement.

"*Almost* everything," Lilah told her. "The meat comes from our son-in-law who raises cattle." She laughed again. "And we know what goes into them because Robert sells him the grain and hay."

Beth ate two platefuls of vegetables and drank three glasses of iced tea. Then, after offering to help clean up, an offer that Lilah politely refused, Beth excused herself and went outside. A few minutes later, after helping her aunt clear the dishes, Delia went outside to look for Beth. She found her curled up in the porch swing on the side porch of the house. She was sound asleep.

Delia sat down on the edge of the porch and looked at Beth's face in repose, glad to have an excuse to look at her without Beth knowing about it.

Impatient with her constant and seemingly compulsive interest in Beth, Delia stood up, her boots scraping the porch. Beth's eyes opened and she scrambled to her feet.

"Is it time to go back to work?" she asked, rubbing her eyes and tucking her grimy T-shirt back into her jeans. She looked down at herself and grimaced. "God, I'm so dirty." She sniffed at herself suspiciously. "Oh, no. I . . . I stink."

Delia grinned and chuckled. "You'll stink a lot worse before the day is over."

Beth followed her to the truck where Robert was waiting. "You know, that's the first time I've seen you smile or laugh since I arrived."

Delia hoisted herself on the back of the truck bed and slid over to make room for Beth. She called to Neji who bounded happily into the truck.

"Why don't you smile or laugh more often?" Beth asked persistently. She lowered her voice. "You have a great smile."

Delia flushed at the long-forgotten pleasure that came from hearing a woman's compliments. Even if the woman was abrasive and had a dirty mouth. She looked at Beth swing from side to side with the motion of the truck as it bounced across the rutted field. She had an easy physical grace that, despite her infuriating personality, appealed to Delia. So, you don't like *her,* just her body, Delia chided herself.

As she always did when placed between two humans, Neji stared straight ahead. Delia watched as Beth put her arm around Neji and scratched behind her ears.

"I can't believe she lets you do that," Delia said. "I've never seen her let anyone do that — at least someone she didn't know."

Beth smiled and took Neji's massive head in her hands. "Dogs love people who love them. Don't they, Neji?"

Delia shook her head at this seemingly nonsensical statement and decided she would never understand dogs or Beth Collins.

By mid-afternoon, even Neji had wilted; she gave up chasing mice and rabbits and took refuge from the sun under the flatbed truck. Delia watched Beth carefully for any sign that she might collapse from the grueling labor, but Beth, though she had slowed down as the day wore on, continued to work steadily. When Beth was lifting the bales onto the truck, her sweat-stained T-shirt rolled up on her arms, Delia could clearly see the ripple of well-defined muscles under her tanned skin. Beth was strong, and more important, she had endurance.

By the end of the day, all of them were exhausted, dirty and famished. On the way back to the house, both women lay face up on the canvas that covered the bales, their faces turned blood red from the last rays of the setting sun. Delia noticed that Beth was still wearing her gloves.

"I'm afraid to take off my gloves and look at my hands," Beth explained when Delia asked her about it. "They feel like they've been shredded."

Delia nodded. "It doesn't matter how many times

you've done it, it always tears up your hands — even with gloves."

Lilah had fixed chicken with dumplings for dinner and she added extra helpings of vegetables and a large tossed salad for Beth's benefit. Cooling on the counter was a homemade peach cobbler. As they ate, Robert announced that he didn't need their help the next day.

"We've got most of it done," he said.

"Well, at least stay tonight," Lilah said. "You're too tired to drive all that way. I cleaned up the little house. There's a pot of hot water on the stove, enough to wash up in."

"Thanks," Delia said. "I think we will stay. I'm pretty sure Nick and Lou checked on the animals today if they drove by and didn't see my truck there." She loaded her plate with another helping of tossed salad. "Even if they didn't for some reason, I know Nick. He probably left them enough for two days."

After her second piece of cobbler topped with vanilla ice cream, Delia wiped her mouth with her napkin and looked over at Beth who was nodding over her plate, much of her food left uneaten. Though they had washed at the basin by the back door, Beth's face was still streaked with dirt and pieces of alfalfa were stuck in her hair. Looking at Beth now, Delia found it hard to believe she was looking at the same fashionably dressed, beautifully coiffed woman she had met in Wixsteader's just twenty-four hours ago.

Delia stood up. "Okay. I think we're going to turn in now." She put her hand under Beth's elbow and helped her to her feet. "She's about to fall asleep in her food."

Both women thanked Lilah, and they walked together in companionable, if weary, silence, Neji padding at their side. The scene the kerosene lantern illuminated was considerably cheerier than the previous night. The cabin was spotless. Lilah had spread a clean tablecloth over the wobbly table and their cots were made up with sheets, blankets and pillows. The small kerosene stove emitted a warmth that eliminated the damp mustiness. A washbasin and a bar of soap and clean towels were laid out on the table.

"Hey, your aunt really did clean up in here," Beth said appreciatively.

"I'm going to get Neji some water and then sit outside on the porch for a while."

Beth grinned. "Don't leave on my account. I'm not modest."

"Well, I am," Delia told her.

Beth shrugged. "Suit yourself."

As she sat on the porch, Delia thought back to how tirelessly and uncomplainingly Beth had worked during the day. She wondered again where the callouses on her hands had come from and what she did to stay in shape. Delia admitted to an ambivalence that she now tried to analyze.

On the one hand, she was still angry with the woman for intruding on her privacy, for complaining about the cabin, the dirt, for her incessant questions, for lecturing her and her aunt and uncle on their diet. On the other hand, Beth had proven herself to be a tireless, uncomplaining worker — a characteristic that Delia admired. And, she grudgingly admitted, she was even starting to like Beth's teasing.

Thinking about her now, Delia wondered what it would be like to bury her hands in Beth's hair, that incredible shining wonder, to feel it cascade across her hands. Unlike the previous evening, Delia no longer felt inclined to dismiss such thoughts from her mind. Though she would never tell Beth, she enjoyed the way Beth flirted with her.

She could hear her now inside the cabin splashing and imagined her standing nude, her strong, lithe body shining in the soft lamplight.

Suddenly, she admitted to herself that she didn't want Beth to leave. She wanted to spend more time with her. Even if it meant arguing and sparring with her. And there was no denying that she could use the money. Especially the sum that Beth had offered. She looked down at Neji who lay beside her and said, "You're a good judge of character. What do you think?"

Neji answered with an enthusiastic bark and Delia stood up abruptly and started toward the door of the cabin. Just as she reached the door handle, she heard Beth's voice and after a moment realized that she was talking on the cellular phone. A stab of irrational jealousy pierced her as she guessed that Beth was talking to "Jack," the man who had called her the night before. She stood quietly and listened, feeling guilty for eavesdropping but unable somehow to turn around and leave.

"No, you did good, Jack. I'm serious. Hold steady

and watch the quarterly earnings when they come out tomorrow. I know, but I just can't walk away. It's too important to me. I gotta go now ... no, she won't. But I'll find someone who will. Look, I'm really whipped. Talk to you tomorrow."

After the room had been quiet for a few minutes, Delia called to Neji and they entered the cabin. She saw Beth sitting on the edge of the bunk dressed again in her blue pajamas. She held her hands out in front of her, looking at her palms.

Neji went directly to Beth and nosed her hands. "Oww!" Beth pulled her hands away from the dog.

"What's the matter?" Delia asked.

"My hands are a little raw."

Delia went over to her and picked up her hands and turned them over. They were bleeding, rubbed raw from the leather gloves.

"I'll bandage them," Delia said. "Did you wash them?"

Beth nodded.

Delia found some gauze and tape on a shelf above the stove and while she was there, she put the tea kettle on. She sat down beside Beth on the bed and began to unwrap the gauze. She was uncomfortably aware of the nearness and warmth of the woman. Beth's hair was loose and shining again; a few strands brushed Delia's cheek. Being this close, with Beth's warm hand in hers, Delia was overwhelmed by the scent of her hair, skin and pajamas. Delia realized that she wanted very much to raise the injured hand and touch it gently to her lips. It seemed to her that Beth was sitting closer to her than she really needed to, leaning against her deliberately. Then Beth raised her unbandaged hand to Delia's face and brushed her cheek.

"You know, as infuriating as you are ... I still like being with you."

Delia felt her throat constrict and she swallowed hard. Was this Beth's way of trying to convince her to take her backpacking? As much as she longed to give in, to trust even a little, something inside her held back.

Tearing her gaze away from Beth's, Delia finished knotting the bandage with a tiny jerk. Beth winced and pulled her hand away. "Ouch, that's a little too tight."

"Purely self-defense," Delia muttered, and handed the gauze and tape to Beth. "You can do the left one," she said. She went out onto the porch and threw the water over the porch railing. "I'm going to wash up myself now. Would you mind sitting on the porch for a while?"

Beth looked up at her with a knowing expression. "What's the matter? Are you scared I'll get fresh with you?"

Delia pointed to the door and waited until Beth left. After she finished washing, she pulled on a pair of blue sweatpants and a long sleeved T-shirt with UNIVERSITY OF UTAH emblazoned across the chest. She slipped on her moccasins and went out onto the porch to empty the pan of water.

Beth was just finishing bandaging her hand. She looked up as Delia came out. "Could you give me a hand with this? I've just about got it, but I need somebody to hold this end."

Delia put down the basin, knelt down beside her

and deftly finished the task. Then she retreated to the far end of the porch and watched as Neji went over to Beth and rested her massive brown head on Beth's shoulder.

Beth scratched the dog behind the ears and looked up at Delia. "Look, I didn't mean to insult anyone today — about the meat," she said.

Delia shrugged.

"I was just surprised to see you eating meat."

"Why?" Delia asked.

"I thought educated people knew better," Beth said. "I mean you're the one who speaks eight languages. If you don't worry about yourself, what about your aunt and uncle? I mean, their cholesterol level must be off the chart."

"Mongolians in the Gobi Desert and the Mauri in Africa live exclusively on red meat and dairy products. They have almost no incidence of heart disease or hypertension.'"

"Yeah? Well, this isn't the Gobi Desert or Africa."

"You know it's funny. White, middle-class Americans are the only people in the world who have the luxury of worrying whether what they're eating is good for them. Most people in the world worry about finding *enough* to eat. They eat whatever is available."

"Oh, am I supposed to be insulted by being called a middle-class American?" Beth grinned disarmingly. "Besides, I'm not middle-class — I'm a Yuppie."

"Obviously," Delia replied. "So what's a Yuppie want with a pack trip?"

"Hey, Yuppies like the outdoors as much as the next person," Beth laughed. "Are your aunt and uncle Indians?"

"They're Native Americans," Delia corrected her. "Lilah is Paiute. Robert is half Navajo, half Ute. He grew up on the Navajo reservation in Mexican Hat with my grandmother."

"What about your grandfather?"

"My grandmother left my grandfather after they'd been married a while and went back to the reservation. Robert lived there most of his life."

"Your grandfather — was he Ute?"

"Yes. His name was Robert Ironfoot — because he worked on the railroad and wore heavy hobnail boots. He met my grandmother, Ruth Many Sheep, at a rodeo in Four Corners and they got married."

Beth was gazing at her in rapt interest. "Is there some reason why she's called that?"

"Navajos have a given name — what many of them call a 'white man's name' — and they have a name that identifies them with their mother's clan and then a secret name that hardly anybody knows. Then when you grow up, you get a nickname — sometimes more than one. Anyway, my grandmother is a very wealthy woman on the reservation. She has a lot of sheep — hence her name."

"Why did your grandmother leave your grandfather?"

"He drank," Delia said shortly, her tone indicating that the subject was closed.

"What about your first name?"

Delia smiled. "My father named me after a friend of his — a famous woman explorer — Delia Ackeley. She was the first woman to cross Africa on foot. My father met her in the Brooklyn Museum —" She stopped and smiled sheepishly at Beth. "It's a long story."

Beth laughed. "Like all your stories. Well, why is your name Ironfoot? What was your father's name?"

"I used my father's name — Whittaker — until I was in college and became interested in my Native American heritage. I decided to take my grandmother's name."

"So you're not worried about getting colon cancer from too much red meat," Beth said, returning to the earlier subject. "Or dying of heart disease from clogged up arteries."

Delia shook her head. "I grew up in seventeen different countries. Whatever people put on my plate, I eat — lots of things most people could consider disgusting, sometimes to keep from starving — termites, grubs, lizards, grasshoppers, snakes — anything with protein."

"I would have to be starving to eat a grub," Beth said, wrinkling her nose.

Delia shrugged. "Grubs aren't bad — if you cook them right, they're really pretty good."

Delia found that she could no longer ignore her desire to be closer to Beth. She went over and sat down beside her. "I've made a decision about the backpack trip."

Beth held her eyes. "I know. You won't take me."

"No, I've decided I *will* take you," Delia said. "I don't have any commitments for a couple of weeks and after we haul some hay up to my house tomorrow, I'll be free."

Beth eyed her warily. "What's the catch?"

"There's no catch — just some conditions."

"Like what?"

"Okay, number one — no phone," Delia said firmly.

Beth shook her head. "I can't do that. Jack will —"

"Either the phone stays or we don't go."

Beth looked ready to argue, but after a few seconds of thought said, "Okay. The phone stays. What else?"

"I want some straight answers from you," Delia said seriously, pointing her finger at Beth. "And if I don't get some answers I believe, then I'm not taking you anywhere."

Beth held Delia's gaze. "I don't know what you're talking about," she said.

"Really?" Delia raised an eyebrow. "Well, for one thing, I don't believe that you flew all the way from Chicago on the off-chance I'd take you backpacking. People make reservations for my llama treks months in advance. You're a smart woman, you would know that. Also, for someone who wants to go on a long backpacking trip, you certainly came unprepared. Today you had to borrow some clothes of mine to bale hay in. What did you think you were going to wear ... a polo shirt and Topsiders?"

Beth's expression was unreadable.

"Number two, you say you're a stockbroker and yet you're deeply tanned and you have callouses on both hands. You're strong, you did a good job today. On the other hand, you hate dirt, and you don't like being uncomfortable when you sleep," Delia shrugged. "I don't know. Those things don't add up somehow. If I didn't know better, I'd say you didn't like the outdoors, at least not camping and backpacking. Which brings us to another problem. If you don't like to camp and you can't stand dirt, why do you want me to take you backpacking?"

Beth looked at her now, interested. "Wow! You're really taking off the gloves now. Go on. You haven't talked this much since I've known you."

Delia ignored her remark. "Okay, number three, I assume that you're a lesbian. The women I took on the raft trip were gay. Plus, I just sense that you are."

"Boy, that's some detective work, Sherlock."

Delia ignored Beth's sarcasm and continued. "So, if you're a lesbian, what are you doing talking to 'Jack' every five minutes?"

Beth wagged her finger at Delia. "You've been eavesdropping."

Delia looked at her. "You're the one who intruded on my life, not the other way around. If you really want me to take you on this trip, you better come up with answers to my questions."

"You make this all sound so mysterious — like I'm devious or something," she said easily. "It's really obvious and simple. First, I work with Jack Phillips. We're business partners. We're working together on a big account. He's a little nervous that I've left him."

"Are you personally involved with him?"

"I slept with him a few times a couple years ago." She shrugged. "But I broke it off almost immediately. Now I know what I'm *not* missing. As for my callouses and the tan ... I sail. I have a twenty-four foot sailboat." She paused. "Do you know anything about sailing?"

Delia shrugged. "Not much."

"Well, that's how come I'm tan and calloused. Hauling sails up and down is a hard job."

"Okay," Delia said. "What about the other things I mentioned?"

"Look, I don't know how else to put it," Beth said impatiently. "I really *do* want to backpack. I've been under a lot of stress at work. I had some vacation coming. I wanted to do something different — get away from the city." She paused. "And the reason I don't have any other clothes with me is because you wouldn't let me bring my suitcases. Remember?"

Delia thought a moment. "I guess you can read a map and a compass if you sail, huh?"

Beth nodded vigorously. "You bet. And as you saw for yourself today, I'm in good shape." She flexed her biceps playfully.

"What kind of clothes *did* you bring? Anything you can wear in the woods?"

"I have a couple pairs of jeans and some sweatshirts."

"Do you have any hiking boots?"

"No," Beth said. "I didn't know what to buy. I figured whatever I needed I could buy once I got out here."

"Okay," Delia said. "Tomorrow we'll go over to Harrison to the sporting goods store and buy you some clothes. Do you have T-shirts — long-sleeved ones? Like long underwear shirts?"

Beth snapped her fingers in mock disappointment. "Nope, sorry. Fresh out of long underwear shirts."

"Well you need some. You don't need a backpack, we'll take one of the llamas to pack our gear, but you'll need a fanny pack. And you'll need a hat."

Beth grinned up at her. "I want one like yours. It looks like the kind of hat Ernest Hemingway used to wear in all those old pictures. All you need is a daiquiri with a paper umbrella."

Delia touched the soft leather brim of her hat. "It was my dad's. He was killed in a plane crash in Africa in 'seventy-five." Delia blinked back a sudden sting of tears.

"I saw a picture of you once about six or seven years ago in a magazine," Beth said. "It was taken in Turkey, I think. You were standing there with that coat billowing all around you and you were holding onto that hat with one hand peering into a dust storm." She looked embarrassed. "I thought you looked so ... romantic. I didn't believe my friends when they told me they'd actually been on a river raft trip and that you were the guide. I'd read about how you sued the university that denied you tenure and there was some rumor about a scandal with a graduate student but then ... there was nothing. What happened?"

Delia's face had grown stony during the last part of Beth's recital. "I ... took some time off," she said finally. "Now, I'm retired. Anyway, most of that stuff in magazines was just media hype. I was never a female Indiana Jones, or whatever it was they called me."

"That's not what it said in *Archaeological Digest*. Said in there you uncovered evidence that, quote, seriously undermined traditional ways of thinking about warrior cultures and women's roles in those societies. Unquote."

Delia looked at Beth skeptically. "You read *Archaeological Digest?*"

"My dentist is an archaeology nut — I just happened to pick it up," Beth said unconvincingly.

Delia nodded. "Uh-huh." She stood up and extended her hands to Beth to pull her up from her sitting position. Beth held out her bandaged hands helplessly.

"These mitts aren't going to be good for anything for a couple of days." Delia grabbed Beth's forearms and pulled her up.

Once Beth was standing she pressed against Delia and put her arms around her waist. "Are you sure you trust yourself alone with me for a week in the wilderness?"

Beth's hair was silky against Delia's cheek, and her breasts yielded against her own. Delia inhaled deeply of the scent that she was beginning to associate only with Beth.

Beth tightened her arms around Delia's waist and kissed her cheek lightly. "I'm really glad you decided to take me," she said sincerely, loosening her arms and stepping back.

Delia savored the warmth and pressure of the embrace and silently wished that it had lasted longer. She wasn't sure how much of her emotions Beth could read from her facial expression.

"Well," she said abruptly. "We'd better get to bed. We'll have a long day ahead of us tomorrow." She opened the cabin door and held it for Beth.

After she extinguished the lantern and stove and climbed into her sleeping bag, Delia tried not to be conscious of Beth's sleeping form across the room. She turned over and over, trying to find a comfortable position on the hard, lumpy mattress. Finally, she gave up and thought over Beth's answers to her probing questions.

She believed most of what Beth had told her. The only trouble she had was with the explanation of why Beth wanted to go on a wilderness trip. The explanation Beth had offered was ludicrous. If she had vacation time coming, why would she choose to take it in the middle of an important business deal?

She dismissed the questions. The actual reason or motivation for why someone wanted to go into the wilderness was irrelevant. As long as she had confidence in Beth's physical ability to walk twenty or thirty miles, there was no reason not to take her. Besides, Delia thought, the extra money Beth was paying her would help subsidize the non-paying customers with whom she would be trekking in a couple of weeks.

A moment later, Delia admitted that money, welcome or not, was hardly the issue. It had been a long time since she had allowed herself to feel desire for someone. She had walled off her emotions, retreated from former friends and colleagues — all reminders of her past life as America's foremost female archaeologist. After the "lost year," as she had come to think of the time that she spent wandering across the country, she had isolated herself by living as far away from media attention as she could get. The Uinta Mountains in the northeastern corner of Utah had been a place where she could ignore the fact that the rest of the world existed. Caring for her llamas, rebuilding the old cabin her father had built at Half Moon Lake over forty years ago, helping Robert on his ranch, spending the winter with her grandmother at Mexican Hat — these activities had filled the huge emotional void that losing her lover, her career, and her friends had left.

Now, only one day after meeting Beth Collins, her peaceful, albeit rather empty, existence was threatened. Delia resolutely turned her back on Beth and closed her eyes. It *was* the money she told herself firmly. It was.

Chapter Four

By late afternoon the next day, Delia and Beth were on their way to Delia's cabin at Half Moon Lake. Their recent purchases from the sporting goods store, along with eight bales of hay, and Neji, were stowed in the truck bed. At the Army surplus store in Harrison they had bought fatigue pants for Beth — the best pants for backpacking, Delia had assured her. "They're roomy, you can tie the cuffs closed — keeps bugs out of your pants leg and they have lots of pockets." At the sporting goods store, Beth had purchased a pair of hiking boots, shorts and a large fanny pack. Beth assured Delia that she had a weatherproof windbreaker.

Delia looked over at Beth dressed in her new corduroy shirt and hiking shorts that showed off her long legs. "You look like you're ready for the mountains now," she assured her.

Beth gestured helplessly. "I feel naked without my telephone and briefcase," she said. "I haven't been without a telephone within arm's reach since — I don't know when."

"You'll get used to it after a few days in the high country," Delia told her confidently. She gestured out the window. "Look at those hills, the sagebrush and the aspens. I love fall in the mountains."

Beth looked out the window at the scattered patches of quaking aspens that dotted the sagebrush-covered foothills surrounding the small town of Harrison; the foothills gradually gave way to the pine, spruce and Douglas fir typical of higher elevations.

"Yes, it's beautiful," Beth said sincerely. "I don't know why I didn't appreciate it before."

"Before what?" Delia asked.

Beth looked away from her. "Oh, nothing," she said, a little sadly. "Before — when I saw it yesterday." She paused. "So, where are we going?"

"Ashley National Forest," Delia told her. "I live in the Uinta Mountains. The Uintas are unique in the United States — they run east-west instead of north-south like the Rockies. They're mostly composed of pre-Cambrian rocks over six hundred million years old." She stopped; Beth was looking at her curiously. "What?"

"Nothing," Beth laughed. "I guess archaeologists know a lot about rocks, geology, stuff like that."

"Sorry," Delia said sheepishly. "Sometimes I forget I'm not in the classroom anymore. Anyway, we're on our way to my home which is on the northern boundary of the forest, not far from Flaming Gorge Reservoir. I live on Half Moon Lake."

"You live in a cabin?" Beth looked at her curiously.

"Yes," Delia said. "My dad bought the land in the forties when he was the chief paleontologist at Dinosaur National Monument. That's where he met my mother."

"At the monument?"

Delia nodded. "My mother lived on the reservation at Whiterocks, where Robert and Lilah live. She worked at the Visitor Center at Dinosaur."

Beth asked with genuine interest, "So why did your father build a cabin in Utah?"

"He loved it here. My dad was from northeast Arkansas — very agricultural. My grandparents still live there. Anyway, it's flat, lots of mosquitoes, very humid. That's why my Dad loved Utah so much — said he dried out for the first time in his life when he lived here. So he bought this land, built a cabin, and when he died the cabin and the land became mine."

The road they were on was gradually worsening. The asphalt surface had given way to a badly graded gravel road that sloped dangerously to the right. Beth looked out across the spectacular vista — golden-leaved aspens shivered among dark green lodgepole pine on the boundary of the basin, and in the distance a long line of snow-capped mountain peaks rose up into a cloudless sky.

Beth said, "You told me yesterday that your mother died when you were six. How did she die?"

"My father and mother were with a French-American expedition in Mongolia — excavating. My mother's appendix ruptured before my father could get her to a hospital."

"God, how awful. What happened to you?"

"I spent a year with my father's parents in Arkansas. I loved them but I was miserable without my father. Finally he came and got me."

"Sounds like you were close to him."

Delia nodded, and the silence that ensued after Beth's last question was a clear indication that she didn't want to talk about her family anymore.

After a short silence Beth asked, "How far is it to your cabin?"

"Not too much further," Delia said, jerking the steering wheel to avoid a gigantic pothole; the truck's right wheel on the passenger side came dangerously close to the edge of the road. Beth gripped the door handle tighter.

The valley below was eventually lost from view as they continued to climb higher. The road grew steadily worse until it was little more than two deeply rutted grooves on either side of a grass-covered ridge that threatened to scrape the underside of the truck.

Two hours later Delia turned off the primitive road and onto an equally primitive dirt track. Neji sat up on her bale of hay and began barking joyously. As they drove the final hundred yards to the house, a small herd of llamas came running through the pasture. Delia slowed the truck as the llamas lined up along the fence, as they always did when she returned home. Near the barn, she could see her two quarter horses, Poppy and Khalid, grazing and, as the truck neared the cabin, Delia's old dachshund, Sam, came waddling slowly down the driveway, barking furiously. A dazzling blue lake shimmered between the lodgepole pines that lined the driveway to Delia's cabin.

"Is that Half Moon Lake behind your house?" Beth asked.

"Yes," Delia said, smiling. "Isn't it beautiful?"

Delia stopped the truck near the barn. Beth rubbed her back which was sore from the long journey and constantly bumpy road.

"That's a helluva road," she remarked, shooting Delia a look. "You don't mind me saying hell, do you?"

Delia, who was busy scratching behind Sam's ears, ignored this piece of sarcasm. Neji had greeted the ancient dog with a peremptory sniff and then bounded off toward the lake. Beth walked a short distance and looked around.

To the right, where the llamas with their long elegant necks stood staring at them, was a red barn with an antique weathervane atop a steeply pitched roof. Numerous other outbuildings were evident further down a hill that sloped away beside the barn. The paddock where the llamas and horses were enclosed was packed dirt and a hayrack and water trough stood in the center of the enclosure. Everything looked well-cared for; the wooden fences freshly whitewashed.

Delia pointed to her log home proudly. "That's my house," she said unnecessarily.

"God, it's beautiful."

Built of logs the color of rich apple butter, the house had a stone chimney in the center of the roof which contrasted nicely with the dark green shingles. A spacious porch formed an L enclosing two sides of the cabin; dark green shutters, closed for the winter, were spaced at intervals around the porch. A pair of cots were set up at the far end of the L and rustic furniture grouped around a round wooden table. Hummingbird feeders and large baskets of blood-red fuchsias hung from the outside rafters of the porch.

Behind the cabin, a windmill turned slowly in the breeze beside a tiny greenhouse whose glass panes winked in the sunlight reflected from the lake. Over the porch a bank of four windows dominated the front of the cabin; above the two center windows a large semi-circular window of stained glass contained a silver half moon and a star above a lone pine tree.

Beth stood looking at the house with wonder, her open mouth an indication of her astonishment. "Wow, pretty impressive."

Delia smiled proudly. "Wait'll you see the front door. I made it myself."

"I can't wait to see the inside." Beth turned away and reached into the back of the truck for her purchases, but Delia shook her head.

"Leave it. I'll introduce you to the llamas and the horses. Then we'll go inside and ..."

Delia never completed her sentence because at

that moment two men emerged from the porch and began walking toward them. Delia turned to Beth to tell her not to be alarmed, she knew the men, but she was stopped cold by the expression of absolute horror on Beth's face.

Chapter Five

Turning back to the two men as they emerged from the shadowy recesses of the porch, Delia greeted her friends, Lou Marcella and Nick Andretti. Both men were dressed in fire-fighting clothes — yellow shirt, dark green pants and aluminum hard hats with the words US FOREST SERVICE stenciled on the front. Their clothes were blackened with soot and ash and Delia smiled as they approached, the smell of their smoky clothing growing stronger.

"Don't worry. I know them," Delia told Beth,

walking over and giving each man a brief hug. "You guys smell. Been over to Flat Top doing that burn?"

Nick Andretti, a short man with dark curly hair and hazel eyes, rubbed his red-rimmed eyes. "Yeah, we burned about ten acres of sagebrush. The Italian Stallion here almost let it get away from us today. Damn near burned down the whole forest."

His companion shoved him playfully. "Ever since we were kids, he screws up, he blames me." He grinned at Delia. "We did just about blow it. The wind shifted all of a sudden and we burned down about three acres of lodgepole."

"Where's your truck?" Delia asked, looking around.

"Oh, the damn thing broke down about three miles from here," Lou said. "I think the generator is shot. It's gonna need a new part. And the radio's on the blink too, so we couldn't call anyone."

"Well, you know I don't have a phone," Delia reminded them. "You could try to rouse somebody on my CB."

"Naw, it doesn't matter," Nick said. "Nobody's expecting us till tomorrow anyway. We were hoping we could con you out of a couple of beers and a place to sleep. We'll hike down to the ranger station at Horseshoe Bend tomorrow morning. Right now we're both so damn tired, we can't walk another step."

During this interchange, Delia noticed that Nick had nodded familiarly to Beth and was now approaching her with a smile. She also noted that the look of dismay on Beth's face had not altered. Beth looked so shaken that Delia half expected her to bolt for the forest behind her. This was a side to Beth Collins that she had not seen before, and she was curious as to what had provoked the reaction.

Nick offered her his hand, and strangely Beth pulled back from him. Nick glanced at Delia with a puzzled expression. "Nice to see you again, Ms. Collins. Maybe you don't remember me — Nick Andretti? We met in the District Office the other day." He paused, waiting for her to respond. When Beth remained silent, he spread his hands.

"You were there asking about your friend — what was her name again?"

Beth's eyes darted around helplessly and when she saw the baffled expression on Delia's face, she turned back to Nick. "Jill. Jill Davis," she said softly.

"Yeah," Nick said. "Jill Davis. I'm sorry I don't remember her. I can't keep track of all the seasonals — especially the ones not in my district." He turned to Lou. "Lou's a seasonal. He might've known her."

Lou shook his head. "The regional guys already asked me. I remember meeting her once over in Manila at the fire school a couple summers ago. But I didn't ever talk to her. We worked in different districts." He turned to Beth. "Has she still not turned up? What's it been now? Six, seven weeks? She must have disappeared right after she got here."

"She worked longer than most seasonals," Beth told them. "She started in May and usually worked until late October, early November. In the winter, she's a ski instructor in Park City." Beth glanced over at Delia whose expression had transformed from one of bewilderment to anger.

"So," Nick continued, oblivious of the tension

62

between the two women, "what's up here? Have you two figured out what happened to her? You know, I never did get the whole story on it. Some people I talked to said she quit, that she'd gotten another job in Montana. Some people in Fish and Wildlife said she just didn't show up for work, never told anyone anything." He looked from Delia to Beth and, getting no response, continued, "Did they ever find her truck?"

Beth shook her head. "No."

"Some guys from the Regional Office nosed around for a few days. But I don't think they found anything," Nick offered. "I think they were satisfied that she just split."

"Will someone please tell me what in the hell is going on?" Delia asked in a voice barely under control.

"It's really nothing," Beth said hurriedly. "I was going to tell you ..."

Nick looked back and forth between the two women. "So are you two friends or what?"

"Nick, why don't you and Lou get a couple beers out of the fridge and sit on the deck while I talk to Beth for a minute. Okay?" Delia asked.

She took both men by the arm and started walking them toward the house. "After we talk, I'll throw some steaks on the grill, okay?"

Nick and Lou brightened at the prospect of cold beer, and after they had gone into the house again, Delia turned to face Beth who had paled under her tan.

"I'm sorry ..." Beth began. "Honestly, I was going to tell you about Jill but I ..."

Delia grabbed Beth's elbow and led her toward

the steps leading up to the front porch. She pushed her none too gently down onto the steps and pointed her finger at her. "You lied to me."

"I didn't lie to you," Beth countered. "I just didn't tell you the whole story."

"All right," Delia snapped. "I want some simple facts. I don't want rationalizations or apologies or explanations. What's going on here? Who's Jill Davis?"

"Jill Davis is my friend. She works for the Forest Service as a seasonal employee."

"What's this about her disappearing?"

Beth took a deep breath and looked off in the direction of the woods. "About six weeks ago, Jill didn't show up for work Monday morning. When she hadn't shown for three days, the Forest Service sent someone over to her trailer and found her truck was gone." Beth looked up at Delia. "Nobody's seen her since."

"Didn't the Forest Service investigate?"

"Not so you'd notice," Beth said bitterly. "Nothing else in her trailer was missing — except her four-hundred-dollar binoculars and a Nikon camera. They assume she was wearing her uniform since it was gone along with her daypack and her canteen. But her other belongings — papers, books — were still there."

"So what do they think happened to her?"

"The ranger in the Bittercreek Office told me they don't think anything happened to her. He said, and the District Ranger repeated it to me, that Jill was a malcontent, a troublemaker. That she had been telling her co-workers for weeks she was dissatisfied with her job, she was looking for another one, that she'd found another one —" She shrugged. "They think she just left without telling them she was quitting."

"How did you find out she had disappeared?"

"I'm listed on her personnel card as being the person to notify in case of an emergency. After Jill was gone a week, her supervisor, the ranger in the Bittercreek office, called me, told me what happened, asked if I had any idea where she might be. Jill doesn't have any close relatives. Her mother died about fifteen years ago, and her father left her mother when Jill was a baby. She doesn't have any aunts or uncles or cousins that she knows of. Just me."

Delia looked at her impatiently. "What's this got to do with me?"

"I told the ranger over the phone what I knew, what her last letter to me had said. He told me he'd be back in touch if they needed anything else. When he didn't call or respond to my phone messages, I flew out here to see what's going on, look through her belongings."

"That doesn't answer my question. Why did you want me to take you on a pack trip?" She demanded, "Why did you lie to me?"

Beth looked away from her. "Jill wouldn't just pull up and leave without telling me. She wouldn't leave all her things either."

Through gritted teeth Delia said, "I repeat — what do you need me for?"

Beth's voice rose. "She works for the wildlife biologist in Bittercreek. In the last letter I got from her, Jill mentioned something about a wildlife camera she goes to check every week or so. The

65

camera's on Ute mountain. Apparently very isolated.
I want you to take me there."

"*Why?*" Delia yelled.

"I want to look for her," Beth yelled back. "I
think something's happened to her."

Delia sat quietly for a moment, digesting the
information Beth had provided. Finally she stood up.
"We're going to eat dinner with Nick and Lou.
Tomorrow morning I'm taking Nick and Lou to
Horseshoe Bend and after that I'm taking you back
to Bittercreek."

Beth opened her mouth to protest, but Delia held
up her hand. "You lied to me. I gave you every
chance to tell me the truth and you lied to me. As
far as I'm concerned, you're already gone." She
turned on her heel and disappeared around the
corner of the house.

Dinner was a strained and silent affair. Delia
cooked thick venison steaks, foil-wrapped baked
potatoes and sweet corn over an open barbecue pit
in the side yard. As she cooked, Delia offered the
terse explanation that Beth had been given her
name by some mutual friends in Chicago who had
thought that she might know something about Jill
Davis's disappearance. During the offering of this
explanation, Delia violently speared a steak, causing
bloody juices to run down into the fire.

"I've explained to Beth that I don't know
anything about it and can't help," she said firmly.
"Tomorrow after I run you and Lou down to the
ranger station, I'll take Beth back to Bittercreek."

Neither man, nor Beth, had any response to this grim announcement and after the remains of dinner had been cleared away, Nick and Lou went off to take showers.

After the men were gone, Delia found Beth slumped in a chair at the far end of the front porch, a half-empty bottle of beer in her hand. Even though she was still extremely angry at Beth, Delia nonetheless marveled at how the sight of a woman she had known for less than forty-eight hours could stir her so deeply. Beth's hair, shining like burnished copper in the last rays of the setting sun, hid her face. Impulsively, something in Delia longed to go to her, but the recognition of such feelings made her angrier at herself than at Beth.

"I'm going to check on my animals," Delia announced abruptly, then strode away when Beth failed to look up.

As she cleaned out the stables and pitched down fresh hay from the hayloft, Delia thought about the strange story that Nick and Beth had revealed that afternoon. Part of her wanted to know more about Beth's friend who had disappeared. Why had the Forest Service not investigated her disappearance more thoroughly? Why did Beth think Jill hadn't just quit her job without telling anyone? Had Jill really been a troublemaker and a complainer? And why had Beth not simply told her the truth from the beginning? All these questions raced through her mind as she worked, her anger making her movements more energetic than she really felt after the long day.

When the llamas saw Delia dip into the grain sack, they bounded into the barn and crowded around the feed pan, pushing and butting each other out of the way. Delia stood back and watched them affectionately. Her favorite llama, Cuzco, a dapple-brown female with a piquant face, came over and nibbled on Delia's shirt buttons. Delia had raised Cuzco from a bottle when her mother was attacked by dogs three years before.

She scratched the llama behind her ears. She had eight llamas in a rainbow of colors — dappled reddish brown, butterscotch, black velvet and snowy white. All were quality animals and two, Harriet and Shasta, had taken awards in llama shows. The llamas were ideally suited to packing in the mountains; their hemoglobin took in more oxygen and carried it twice as long as humans. A fully mature female could carry fifty to seventy pounds twenty miles a day for three weeks. Delia smiled wryly; *will carry* was a more accurate phrase. If a llama was overpacked with more weight than it felt like carrying, it would simply lie down in the trail and not budge until the extra baggage was removed.

As she brushed Cuzco, Delia's anger at Beth smoldered. She thought back to their conversation on the porch at Robert's the night before, remembered Beth's assurances that she was telling her the truth, her flirtatious manner; and Delia felt her anger surge up again. The warm barnyard smells of hay, horses and llama wool usually calmed and soothed her tensions away, but her anger was so acute that she could think of nothing but Beth's betrayal. To be fair to Beth, Delia admitted, a good deal of her anger was tied up with her feelings about Robin; the pain of Robin's betrayal — so public and so catastrophic for Delia's career — was buried deep, through years of practice. The fact that she had let herself feel something for Beth, that she had let her guard down even a little, only to be lied to, was particularly painful.

It was dark when Delia walked back to the cabin and the night air was chilly. Hearing a movement off to her left, she stopped and waited until she saw Neji coming through the stand of trees that lined the road. She rested her hand on Neji's huge head and stepped up onto the porch. She could hear the murmur of voices from inside, an occasional burst of laughter from Nick. She thought back to Beth's dejected attitude on the porch earlier. Although she had seemed defeated and depressed, Delia knew, even from her brief acquaintance with Beth, that she was not a woman to give up easily. She had gotten Delia to offer her a place to stay the first night they met, had ignored Delia's initial refusal to take her backpacking and within twenty-four hours had convinced her to change her mind. There was little doubt in Delia's mind that having come this far, Beth would not simply give up.

As she opened the door to her cabin, Delia grimly vowed to herself that she would not give Beth the opportunity to talk her into anything.

Delia awakened in the middle of the night. The loft that served as her bedroom was an addition that she and Shawla had added after they had begun the job of restoring the cabin after thirty years of neglect. The stained glass window with its pine tree, half moon and star, cast misshapen shadows on the thick Navajo rugs covering the floor of the loft. Delia remembered the day she had seen the cabin for the first time: the roof was rotted through and as a result the interior had suffered extensive damage. The floorboards were warped and rotted; one wall had to be entirely rebuilt.

Delia kicked off one of the blankets. The heat from the woodstove heated her lofty bedroom almost too efficiently some nights. Turning over on her back, she stared up into the shadowy beams of the ceiling above her. She noticed that Neji wasn't sleeping by the bed and wondered where the dog was. She didn't wonder for long, however; she heard the murmur of Beth's voice and Neji's answering woofs and grunts from the living room beneath her. Nick and Lou were bedding down on the front porch on the two cots, snug in down sleeping bags. After the two men had retired to the front porch, Beth had sarcastically offered to sleep in the barn. After throwing down a pillow and blankets from the loft, Delia had retorted, "Don't tempt me."

Those were the only words the two women had exchanged since their heated exchange that afternoon.

Curious in spite of herself as to what Beth was saying to Neji, Delia got up and slipped into her flannel robe and moccasins. She moved closer to the railing and looked down into the living room where Beth was talking to Neji.

"I screwed up, Neji," Beth confided softly. "I shouldn't have lied to her." She paused. "Ah, hell, I know the whole thing sounds so farfetched. I knew nobody else would understand or believe it. But dammit, I *know* something's wrong. And I know Jill's up there somewhere, maybe sick or hurt. I'm the only one who knows she needs help."

Beth stroked the dog's massive head which was resting in her lap. "I only lied because I thought she wouldn't help me ..."

Despite her anger and hurt at Beth's deception, Delia was moved by the tenderness in Beth's voice when she spoke of her friend. Delia stopped in mid-thought. She had assumed that Jill was Beth's friend. Could she have been her lover?

In spite of her vow not to even consider helping her again, Delia found her admiration for Beth's stubborn persistence increasing. She knew that her refusal to take Beth to Ute Mountain to search for her friend would not prevent Beth from accomplishing what she had traveled so far to do.

Delia sat down heavily on the edge of the bed and sighed. What she contemplated went against every instinct and ounce of reason she possessed. From the first moment she had seen Beth Collins, she had tried to say no to her, had tried to somehow extricate herself from becoming involved with her. But as strong as the instincts were which told her to pull away, something even stronger drew her to Beth.

Delia stood up. She made no effort to be quiet; she could still hear Beth's low murmuring and Neji's muffled responses. She walked resignedly down the narrow wooden steps that led from the loft to the front room.

Beth looked up in surprise when she saw Delia. Neither woman spoke for a few minutes and then Delia smiled wearily.

"Okay, let's try this one more time. I have some

questions for you and you'd better answer them truthfully or I won't help you."

Beth patted the couch beside her. "No problem. I'll put another log on the fire."

Chapter Six

Two days later Delia and Beth were bouncing down another bad gravel road on their way to Ute Mountain. They pulled a small horse trailer that housed the largest of Delia's llamas, Cuzco. Also in the bed of the pickup were the specially made nylon packs containing the food and equipment they would need over the next week.

After talking to Beth and studying the topographical map of Ute Mountain that Beth had found in Jill's trailer, Delia had agreed to a one-week pack trip. She and Beth had talked for a long time, Beth telling Delia about her relationship with Jill Davis and the circumstances surrounding her disappearance. It was evident from the way Beth talked about Jill that night that she still cared very deeply about her former lover.

"Even though we broke up almost six years ago, we're still close," Beth had explained. "I know Jill, she'd never go off and not tell me."

"Would it be like her to quit her job without giving notice?"

"Well, it wouldn't surprise me. Jill's a hothead. Even more than I am. I used to call her 'Hotdog' because she always wanted to do things dramatically, get people's attention. And she had talked about quitting. She was having a lot of trouble with her job. She was out at work and some of the people who worked around her didn't like it. But she wouldn't leave her job without telling me where she was going."

"So what do you think happened to her?" Delia asked.

"I don't know," Beth admitted. "That's why I want to go to Ute Mountain."

Beth went on to explain that Jill had mentioned in a letter that she intended to go change the film in the wildlife camera on Ute Mountain the weekend before she disappeared.

"What sort of wildlife camera?" Delia asked.

"According to Jill's letters, the Forest Service built a watering trough on Ute Mountain a couple of summers ago. It was one of the wildlife projects that Jill worked on. They transplanted some mountain sheep from Wyoming up there. Anyway they have a video camera rigged up at the trough that's tripped whenever an animal drinks out of it. I guess they keep track of animal populations that way."

"Why would Jill go up there on a weekend?"

"She was always doing work stuff on her own time," Beth said. "She worked twice as hard as everybody else. She felt like she always had to prove herself."

"Do you know exactly where this camera is located?" Delia asked.

"When I went through Jill's papers at her trailer — I have her stuff in the trunk of the rental car — I found a topographical map with a trail marked out in red — she had the camera's location marked."

"I wonder why she didn't take it with her," Delia mused.

Beth shrugged. "I wondered that too. Maybe she knew the area well enough that she didn't need a map. Or maybe this was an old map, from when she helped build the watering trough last year."

Delia had asked Beth more questions about her friend and their relationship, and Beth had assured Delia that, at least as far as she knew, Jill was not involved with drugs or anything illegal. She and Jill wrote or called each other once a month. Beth bowed her head when Delia asked her if she realized that the odds of finding her friend were extremely slim.

"Yeah," Beth replied. "I know. But it *is* possible, isn't it, that she's been hurt or gotten sick and is still alive up there?"

"It's possible," Delia admitted. "Seven weeks is a long time to be missing. People have gotten lost up in the Uintas and never been found. But it's possible. The hard part is knowing where to look."

"I know it sounds half-assed," Beth conceded.

"But I can't just do nothing. She doesn't have anyone else who cares."

And so when Shawla returned, Delia and Beth were already packed and ready to go. Shawla came back two nights after Delia and Beth had their late-night talk. They were in the barn where Delia was checking the survival kit that she carried in a large belt pack. Beth was watching as Delia laid out the contents of the pack on a large worktable.

"What the hell do you need all that for?" Beth asked, looking over the assortment of items Delia had spread out on the table.

"It's not that much," Delia said. "And it's all important. Even if we lost everything else, the stuff in here would keep us alive indefinitely."

"What's it for?" Beth asked.

"Well, there's a first aid kit — just a little one for emergencies. I have a bigger one in the other pack that Cuzco carries that's more extensive," Delia said. "It has a sterile suture kit, hemostats, scissors, Lomotil, Compazine, Butyn Opthaline Ointment, Sulfasuxidine, Pyridium and an ampule of morphine."

"Sounds like you're planning to open a hospital," Beth muttered. "Why so much?"

"A good first aid kit can save a trip. If you can take a stitch or treat diarrhea or an eye injury, you can keep from having to turn back. Besides, if . . . *when* we find Jill, she might be badly hurt. I want to be prepared for anything. At any rate," Delia said, zipping up the fanny pack, "if something happened and we were stranded up there, we'd be okay as long as we have this." She patted the pack.

"I can think of worse things than being stranded in the wilderness with you," Beth said suddenly, hooking her fingers into Delia's belt. She pulled Delia to her and kissed her.

Delia stood motionless for a moment, then returned the kiss. All the tension of their attraction was released in the kiss. Their mouths crushed together, tongues entwined. They clung together for a long moment then Beth broke away and squeezed Delia.

"Jesus, you can kiss."

They might have ended up on the floor of the barn had they not heard a car coming up the drive.

They moved apart and Delia looked at Beth. "That's probably Shawla." She turned away from Beth and began measuring out grain into a Ziploc bag. Remembering Beth's questions about whether Shawla was her lover, Delia watched Beth's face with amusement when she met her.

A few moments later, a large black woman with iron gray, close-cropped hair entered the pool of light outside the barn entrance. Dressed in blue jeans and a leather jacket, the woman with the cold, alert eyes of a hawk took in Beth and Delia. Delia turned to her and smiled slightly.

When Shawla finally spoke, her voice was rough like the teeth of a saw cutting into a rotten log. "I'm back."

"How was your sister?" Delia asked.

Shawla walked toward them, her limbs moving slowly, almost gingerly, as if she were in great pain though her face revealed nothing. "Fine. Better."

"Good," Delia said shortly. "I'm taking this woman on a pack trip tomorrow. Be back in about a week."

Shawla looked curiously at Beth for a few moments. "When's the next group comin'?"

"Three weeks," Delia answered.

At this Shawla lifted one shaggy black eyebrow and then shrugged. "Okay," she said and, after touching Delia briefly on the shoulder, walked away toward the back of the barn.

A few moments later Beth asked, "Where did she go?"

Delia motioned with her head. "She lives in the back room off the barn." Her tone discouraged further questions about Shawla, or her sister.

The next morning, after loading all their gear into the truck and saying good-bye to Neji and Sam, the two women left without ever seeing Shawla.

"Are we going to follow the route Jill marked on the map?" Beth asked, holding onto the door handle as the truck bounced up and down.

"Yes," said Delia. "It's our only lead, really. If she actually went up there the weekend before she disappeared, we may find something." Delia steered expertly around another pothole. "It's funny. On the map you found, the route Jill marked didn't follow a trail. It's like she plotted a different way with a compass before she left."

"Why would she do that?" Beth asked.

"I don't know. But we're going to have to follow her trail," Delia said. "It'll be harder this way."

"How are we getting back? Just hike back to where we started?"

"No," Delia told her. "Next week Shawla will get a ride over to Bittercreek. Robert will drive her over to Whiskey Basin which is where we'll end up — on the other side of Ute Mountain, near my house. She'll pick us up there."

"Maybe we'll have Jill with us," Beth said.

Delia looked at her. "Yes, hopefully we will."

They drove on, climbing steadily higher all the time. Half Moon Lake dropped away behind them and soon was lost to view as they rounded one hairpin turn after another. The sky was a brilliant blue, and Ute Mountain, snowcapped and majestic, loomed in the distance.

The gravel road eventually gave way to dirt. After an hour or so of bumping and bouncing along, they reached the summit of Windy Ridge Pass and began their descent. At the summit some dirty patches of snow lingered between the tall stands of timber, and the air was crisp, hinting of the winter soon to come. Delia pointed out a small herd of mule deer grazing on a mountainside.

Almost three hours later, they bounced over a wooden bridge that spanned a deep, icy green stream. Delia pulled the truck and trailer off onto a narrow, rutted road, drove a quarter mile and stopped. The truck and trailer faced a meadow ringed with huge Douglas firs and lodgepole pines. Indian paintbrush grew in wild profusion, a last explosion of color and growth before winter.

Delia unloaded Cuzco from the trailer and tied her halter rope to a nearby tree where the llama began grazing placidly. Then she went back to the truck and unsnapped the 30.30 rifle that rested in a specially-made rack behind the seat.

Beth looked at the rifle curiously and, seeing the look, Delia explained. "It was my father's," she said fondly, caressing the worn stock.

"Do you usually take a gun when you go backpacking?"

"Sometimes. I think it would be a good idea this time." She checked the rifle to be sure it was unloaded and leaned it carefully against the side of the truck.

"It's almost noon now," Delia said, looking up at the sun. "We might as well eat a couple of sandwiches before we start. That way we won't have to stop and eat in half an hour."

Afterward, Delia loaded the two packs that contained their food, sleeping bags, cooking utensils and other equipment on Cuzco's back, moving the packs around and making adjustments in the belly and chest bands until they were secure. Delia looked once again at the map that Jill Davis had left.

"Okay," she said. "According to the map, this is the spot where Jill began. The way she mapped it out, it looks like it's uphill all the way. The camera's about twenty five miles from here — it'll probably take three or four days." Delia handed Cuzco's halter rope to Beth. "She'll follow. She only stops if she thinks she's carrying too much."

The two women struck off across the meadow. When they reached its edge, they entered a stand of aspen, still resplendent with quivering gold leaves. Delia found a game trail through the trees and followed it until the aspens gave way to dense pine and Douglas fir. Underneath, pine needles carpeted the forest floor, and sunlight filtered through the trees, warming them. Both women shed their sweaters. By late afternoon, they wore cotton T-shirts.

Delia was encouraged at the pace Beth kept even though her new boots had worn some tender places on her feet. A few times during the day, when they stopped for a handful of trail mix or a drink from the canteen, Delia had Beth take off her boots and apply moleskin to the tender spots. On Delia's advice, Beth had worn the boots for a few hours each day before they left on their trip so the places weren't likely to develop into blisters.

The sun was an orange smear against the low-lying clouds behind Ute Mountain when Delia halted in a small stand of pines beside a shallow stream. With Delia's help, Beth removed the nylon packs and tethered Cuzco to a tree near a small patch of grass and ferns where the llama immediately began to graze.

Beth watched as Delia took a pine bough and swept clear an area between two trees. She removed a piece of plastic groundsheet, a blue tarp and a length of thin nylon cord from the packs. Within minutes Delia had hammered stakes into the ground, looped the nylon cord through the grommets on the tarp and anchored the tarp to the trees and ground.

Beth helped her put the ground cloth underneath the tarp and then they blew up their air mattresses and unrolled their sleeping bags. As they worked, the two women joked and laughed together, the atmosphere between them relaxed and easy.

As Delia arranged stones in a circle for a fire ring, she reflected on the closeness that had developed between them since the first night they had met. It was a volatile closeness, subject to flare-ups sparked by the equally matched natures of two extremely stubborn women. But it was a closeness that grew stronger every day. As she arranged the small twigs and sticks in the stone ring, Delia wondered if Beth felt it as much as she did. She looked up to see Beth bending over to pick up some wood and the sight of her slim yet womanly hips beneath the fabric of the cotton shorts made Delia's stomach tighten.

Beth dumped her load of wood beside the fireplace and squatted down beside Delia. She looked around at the growing darkness. "I don't know why being outside on land makes me so uneasy. I can be out on the water for days and never feel frightened."

"What are you frightened of?" Delia asked.

"Not frightened really. Just uneasy. I don't know. Wild animals?"

"You're safer here than you are in your apartment in Chicago. The only wild animals in the mountains in this area are an occasional black bear and maybe a mountain lion or two." Seeing Beth's expression at this information she added hastily, "But I've never even seen a bear or mountain lion around here. They're very shy."

Delia reached into the pack behind her and pulled out a skillet, a small aluminum pot, and a coffee pot which she handed to Beth. "Get some water from the stream, would you? We'll want hot water to wash up in later."

When Beth came back from the stream, delicious aromas had already begun to drift from the campfire. "Smells good," she said, setting the coffee pot on the ground. "What is it?"

Delia picked up the coffee pot and set it on the wire grill next to the skillet. "I call it cowboy stew," she told her. "It's usually made with hamburger or some kind of meat but I've substituted kidney beans and lentils." She felt slightly embarrassed as she saw the look of appreciation at her thoughtfulness on Beth's face.

Beth leaned over her shoulder and saw an appetizing mixture of vegetables, potatoes and beans bubbling in the skillet. Delia was pleasantly aware of Beth's warm breath on her neck and she felt Beth's hand on her shoulder. "Thanks for the beans."

When dinner was ready, Beth quickly finished off a plateful of the stew, mopping up the remains with a piece of bread and then leisurely ate another plateful until she was forced to loosen the top button of her shorts. When Delia saw Beth begin to rise to help her with the cleanup, she held up her hand. "No need to help," she told her, piling the dirty dishes inside each other and squirting some liquid soap into them. "You paid for a packtrip and that means I do all the cooking and cleaning up afterwards."

Beth leaned back against a log and laced her fingers behind her head. "Hey, what a deal. All I need now is a brandy and a cigar," she joked.

After the dishes were cleaned and put away and all remnants of food were either eaten or buried, Delia went over to check on Cuzco. The llama lifted her head as Delia approached and made a low humming sound in her throat. Delia held out a shallow pan with a cupful of grain and stood quietly while Cuzco ate. Afterward, Delia took the llama and hobbled her a short distance away. She returned to the campfire where Beth was still stretched out in front of the fire.

Sated with food, muscles aching pleasantly, the two women sipped at the decaf Delia had brewed. "Did you mention brandy a while back?" Delia asked.

Beth looked at her with a puzzled expression. "Yeah."

Delia reached into the pack and produced a bottle of brandy, some cocoa powder and evaporated milk.

"I can make campfire Brandy Alexanders. Would you like that?"

"You bet."

Delia measured out a small amount of brandy, cocoa and milk into each cup and stirred the mixture.

Beth sniffed her cup tentatively and took a sip. She looked over the top of her cup at Delia with a surprised expression. "Hey, not bad."

Delia smiled. "Well, it's probably good because we're outdoors." She sipped at her own cup. "My dad used to say that a lot of stuff that we eat with great relish outdoors is stuff we wouldn't touch at home."

Delia nestled back against the nylon packs and sighed deeply. "I love the way the air smells at this altitude. I'd sleep outdoors all the time if I could."

Beth smiled at her over the rim of her cup. "Is that because you grew up in a tent?"

"Probably. I had a hard time when I went to Nairobi for high school. I'd never had to live indoors with other people. I was used to being in a tent of my own or sometimes sleeping under the stars. It's hard."

"Jill's like that too," Beth said. "She loves being outside."

"Were you childhood friends?"

Beth nodded. "We've known each other since the third grade. We went to high school together — even did it once in high school after we both got drunk. Jill's mother was still alive then. She died in a fire when Jill was a senior." Beth paused. "I think we were always a little in love with each other. Then I went away to college, Jill stayed home and took care of her mother, who was alcoholic, until she died. I was her only friend."

"I never had a friend when I was young," Delia confided.

"No friends?" Beth asked incredulously.

"Well, not friends of my own age or sex ... or even race. Most of my friends were the men or women who worked with my father in the field."

"You must have been lonely," Beth said.

"No." Delia shook her head. "Not really." She refilled their coffee cups and added more cocoa, milk and brandy. "I was happy when I was with my father." She smiled. "I don't remember my mother very much. But my grandmother and her sisters — all my mother's relatives — have told me a lot about her."

"Is Shawla from around here?"

The unexpected question caught Delia off guard and she looked up from the flames of the campfire in surprise. "Shawla? No."

"Who is she?"

Delia's reticence to talk about herself and her past was melting away under the influence of the brandy, fatigue and Beth's questions.

"After I lost my job, I kind of had a nervous breakdown. My father was killed, the relationship I was in ended, and then I was denied tenure." Delia paused and poked at the fire with a stick, sending pieces of ash flying up into the darkness. "Everything fell apart — including me."

"You don't have to tell me this if you don't want to," Beth said softly.

"No," Delia said. "I want to. Anyway, it's hard to explain. I sold some of my things, put the rest in storage, took the money in my savings account and got in the car and drove."

"Where did you go?"

Delia shrugged. "I didn't really have a plan. I had it in my head that I would drive to Utah and visit Robert and Lilah. I'd spent some time with them when I was younger. Anyway, it was weird. The further away from my home that I got, the more disoriented I felt. It was like — driving in a dream. Finally, in Kansas City, my car broke down. I'm sure it wasn't anything serious, but I abandoned it."

"Just left it?"

"Yes. I took some things out of my car — some camping things — and left the car on a street in Kansas City. And I started walking."

"How far did you get?"

"Denver," Delia said simply.

"You walked all the way from Kansas City to Denver?" Beth asked in disbelief.

Delia nodded.

"Where did you stay?"

"I camped out."

"Didn't you have any money?"

"Oh, yes, I had money. I kept it in my shoe. But I didn't want to stay in a hotel. It was like I was shedding my skin along the way. Dropping everything. I didn't want to talk to people — even clerks in a hotel, or waitresses. So I cooked my own meals and slept in fields or in the woods. I wore an old pair of pants and my Dad's duster and hat. I found out if you dress and look a certain way, people see through you — like you're not there. Eventually, people didn't talk to me, they acted like they didn't see me." She smiled. "I wore out two pairs of hiking boots."

"Where does Shawla come in?" Beth asked.

"By the time I finally got to Denver I had run out of cash. Ended up living on the streets, picking up cans, eating in soup kitchens or out of garbage cans. I met Shawla on the street one night. I was sleeping in a doorway on Larimer Street — some kids jumped me and tried to take my clothes. Shawla came by and —" Delia stopped and smiled. "Well, she kicked their butts, to put it mildly. We became friends." Delia drained her cup and set it on the ground. "Anyway, a few months after we met, Robert found me. We went to my grandmother's place in Mexican Hat for a while, then I went back to Denver, got Shawla and we came here." Delia looked at Beth. "End of story."

"Wait a minute," Beth protested. "How did Robert find you? How did you find Shawla again? Why did you bring her here? And why in the hell does she live in your barn?"

Delia smiled. "It's a —"

"Long story," Beth finished. "I know, I know."

"Shawla lives in the barn because she wants to. She's a very private person; she didn't want to live with me in the cabin. While we were building the barn, she asked me if I wanted her to stay after all the remodeling was finished. I said yes. She said if she was staying she wanted her own room and could she build a room on the back of the barn. I said yes. So she did."

"It seems like your aunt and uncle don't like her," Beth remarked.

"It's not that they don't like her," Delia said. "They just don't understand our relationship." Delia poked at the fire again. "I don't either, I guess. We aren't and never have been lovers. We don't even talk that much. We're just ... bonded somehow — on a level that I've never been bonded with anyone else." Delia stared into the fire for a long moment. "One day while we were putting a new roof on the house she told me her husband and two kids were killed when their trailer burned down."

"Jesus," Beth whispered, thinking back to the hard, dark eyes of the woman. "What's all this about a sister in Salt Lake?"

"I don't know," Delia said. "But every so often she goes to Salt Lake for a few days. I've never asked her what she does. She may drink, or get laid or go to church. I don't know. I figure if she wants me to know, she'll tell me."

"Well, maybe she does have a sister in Salt Lake," Beth offered.

They fell silent then and listened to the crackle of the fire and the wind soughing high in the treetops. The circle of light and warmth and the soothing sound of the stream surrounded them.

Delia finished her cup of coffee and noticed Beth had finished too. She reached out for her empty cup and when their hands touched, Delia stopped and looked into Beth's eyes. There, she saw a reflection of herself and her own desire. Beth's fingers closed around Delia's and the silence and loneliness that Delia had nurtured for five years bore down on her with a terrible sudden weight. She watched as Beth set her coffee cup down on the ground, never breaking the contact of their hands.

Slowly, she reached for Beth's other hand and pulled her to her feet. As she put her arms around Beth, a surge of vitality and power coursed through her. She put her hands on either side of Beth's face, feeling her hair, soft and luxurious under her palms. Bringing Beth's face close to her, she leaned forward and their lips met.

Tentatively at first, she pressed her lips against Beth's, leaning into the kiss, their tongues pushing into each other's mouths. As Beth's strong hands worked their way up Delia's arms, kneading and caressing in rhythm with their mouths, Delia felt waves of desire break over her and she began unbuttoning Beth's shirt, pushing it down her smooth shoulders. She kissed Beth's neck and shoulders, and Beth moaned.

Suddenly, Delia pulled away and backed up. Beth stared at her, stunned by the abrupt break in their contact.

"What's the matter?" she asked hoarsely, pulling her shirt up over her breasts.

Delia shook her head miserably. She turned her back on Beth, hating herself, unable to look at Beth.

"Don't you want this?" Beth asked.

Delia shook her head and walked a few paces away from the warmth of the fire and the passion that still smoldered in her.

"It's not you, it's me."

"I don't get it," Beth said. "I thought — don't you want to make love with me?"

Delia turned around and regretted it immediately. Beth's fierce beauty pierced her and she longed to kiss her again.

"You know I do," Delia told her. "But I —"

"Is there someone else?"

Delia lowered her eyes to the fire. The embers glowed fiercely, their dying light reflected on Beth's face. She wanted to tell Beth about Robin and for a moment it felt as though the whole sad story would come spilling out of her, just as, a few moments before, the story about her and Shawla had come spilling out.

Suddenly, and surprisingly after so many years, Delia really did want to share the hurt that Robin's betrayal had left her with. But she couldn't.

Delia checked on Cuzco for one last time and as she stood next to the comforting warmth and smell of the llama, she was overcome with sadness and buried her face in the animal warmth of Cuzco's wool. Tears burned her eyes, but she shook her head furiously. Self-pity had never been one of her failings and she didn't intend to start indulging herself now.

Later, when they were in their sleeping bags, Beth, her head resting on her hand, asked, "Do you think there's any chance — any chance at all — that we might find her?"

"I don't know," Delia admitted. "If the letter Jill sent you about coming to Ute Mountain was right, and if she actually went up there using the route marked on the map, then I'd say we have a chance."

"I can't explain it but I just have a feeling she's up here somewhere." She sighed. "I know it's not much but it's all I have."

"We better get to sleep," Delia said. "We've got a long way to go tomorrow." She made a pillow by rolling up her clothes and advised Beth to do the same.

"Goodnight, Dee," Beth said softly.

Delia lay awake for a long time, unable to sleep. Her mind went over the kiss she and Beth had shared, savoring it, and part of her wanted to wake Beth up and take her in her arms again. Finally fatigue conquered her and, still thinking of how soft and warm Beth's lips had been beneath her own, she too slept.

Chapter Seven

The next morning Delia spread out Jill's map on the ground, anchoring each corner with stones.

"Here's where we are," she said, pointing. "It'll probably take us another two days to reach the wildlife camera, it's on the other side of the mountain. When we get above ten thousand feet or so — maybe not even that high — you may have some trouble getting your breath or have headaches. And remember too, if you start getting a sore spot on your feet, be sure and tell me. We can put more moleskin on or you can switch to your running shoes for a while."

After Beth gave Cuzco a handful of grain and half of her breakfast apple, the two women started off. The terrain grew more rugged with every mile and at mid-morning they stopped at the base of an enormous boulder field.

Beth squinted at the huge boulders whose seams of quartz reflected the morning sunlight. "God, they're as big as houses," she exclaimed. "We'll never be able to climb over them."

"I don't understand why in the world Jill would come this way." Delia paused. "This morning while I was looking at the map, I found an abandoned logging trail on the other side of the mountain which would have led her directly to the camera."

Beth tugged on the halter lead and drew Cuzco closer to her. She put her face alongside the llama's and rubbed her cheek against the llama's rough outer coat. Delia smiled. Beth had the same warm rapport with the llama that she'd had with Neji. She remembered Beth's disappointment when Delia explained that she rarely took Neji on backpacking trips with her.

"Why not?" Beth had asked. Neji sat at her side, looking up at Beth as if glad that at last someone was around to speak up for her.

"A couple of reasons," Delia explained. "Number one, she eats too much. I'd have to take a fifty-pound bag of food if she went. Number two, she runs around and chases everything — chipmunks, deer, pikas, weasels, and —" Delia had looked at Neji meaningfully, "skunks!"

Beth wriggled her nose. "Skunks?"

Neji lowered her eyes to the ground at this word, as if embarrassed by the shameful reminder.

"Believe me," Delia said. "You do not want to be around her after she has misjudged the temperament of a skunk."

Beth had not protested anymore, but Neji had sulked for days before they left, as she always did when she sensed Delia was going somewhere without her.

Now Delia watched as Beth checked the belly and chest bands on Cuzco's packs and scratched the animal affectionately behind her erect ears.

"Let's sit down a minute and eat something and decide which way would be the best to go," Delia suggested.

As they ate their oranges, Delia considered their options aloud. "No matter which way we go, we're going to be in pretty rough country from now on," she said around an orange section that Beth had put in her mouth. She felt touched by the intimate gesture and remembered once again, as she had periodically throughout the morning, the kiss they had shared the night before. "A lot of talus slopes, boulder fields, glacier lakes. The camera's located near a deep canyon too — there's a river at the bottom that eventually flows into the Green." She looked up at Beth who was studying the map intently too. "Any way you look at it, it's going to be tough going."

Beth looked at her directly, her blue eyes serious. "Are you trying to tell me that if I want to turn back, now's the time to do it?"

Delia smiled faintly. "For someone who doesn't know me very well, you know me pretty well."

"I feel like I know you," Beth said, removing a stray piece of orange at the corner of Delia's lips. "I thought I was getting to know you better last night. That was a pretty hot kiss."

Delia felt her face flush, and she hastily folded the map, stood up and stuffed the map into the side pocket of her fatigue pants. She put her hat back on and looked up at the sun.

"We'd better be going. The sun will go down quicker at this elevation, and we'll get more tired sooner."

Beth put the orange rinds into a plastic sack and put them in her day pack. Delia watched with satisfaction; she was pleased that, unlike many other clients, Beth was a naturally tidy person, not leaving things around for others to pick up. When Delia had explained to her about burying her own waste and handed her a small trowel, Beth had accepted it matter-of-factly.

It took them the better part of the afternoon to skirt the boulder field. Delia identified the animals — maromets, pikas and chipmunks — that made their home among the boulders. She also identified for Beth the wild columbines often found growing along the hundreds of thin icy waterfalls that flowed from the glacier fields above them.

"We may see some of the mountain sheep they transplanted up here," Delia told Beth. "We might see elk or deer too. If you keep your eyes open, you might see beavers."

"You're a regular Marlin Perkins, aren't you?"

Beth teased, pulling Delia's hat down over her eyes. "I feel like I'm on *Wild Kingdom.*"

Delia found another game trail through the dense forest. As they climbed higher, the air grew chilly and thin.

When they finally stopped for the night, Delia noticed that Beth looked exhausted. "Are you all right?" she asked as she lit the burner of the camp stove.

"I have a ferocious headache," Beth admitted. "Feel a little queasy."

"It's probably the altitude," Delia said, digging into her fanny pack. She shook out two aspirin. "I'll have some tea ready in a minute. Why don't you go lie down while I make something to eat?"

Beth retreated under the tarp without protest, an indication, Delia decided, of both how tired she was and how much her head hurt. Delia knew the aspirin would work within a half hour and with hot food in her, Beth would be fine. Nevertheless, Beth's painful expression made her want to ease her discomfort.

After she started dinner, Delia dug down into the pack and pulled out the canvas duster that had belonged to her father. She wrapped it around Beth who had come out from under the tarp and joined her by the fire. To Delia's relief, she looked better.

"Headache gone?" Delia asked as she stirred the contents of the skillet.

Beth nodded. "Dinner smells terrific. What is it?"

"Vegetarian spaghetti."

The spicy smell of the spaghetti stimulated the appetites of both women. Delia cut thick slices of sourdough bread and lined each plate, pouring the spaghetti sauce over the bread. She shook a generous measure of Parmesan cheese over each serving and handed Beth her plate.

As they ate Delia noticed that the color was coming back into Beth's cheeks, and the pain that had creased her forehead was gone. After Delia cleaned up the dishes, she poured each of them a cup of strong tea.

"The caffeine in the tea will help your headache and nausea."

The small fire crackled and bathed the two women in its warmth. They sat together in companionable silence, shoulders touching, listening to the night sounds all around them. Eventually Beth put her head on Delia's shoulder, and, unlike the previous night, when she took Delia's face in her hands and kissed her, Delia returned her kiss with fierce passionate abandon.

Beth drew Delia inside the warm coat which was big enough for them both. They kissed each other with all the pent-up passion of two people who had denied their attraction to each other for too long.

Delia reveled in the feel and scent of Beth's hair and between kisses she ran her hands through it, marveling again at its shining softness. She pulled off Beth's sweater and unbuttoned her shirt, slipping it off her shoulders and pushing it down around her waist. She ran her hands slowly over Beth's breasts, her palms caressing their smooth contours, and delicate, hardened nipples. Beth groaned with pleasure and murmured Delia's name as Delia took each nipple in her mouth in turn, teasing it, flicking it gently with her tongue. She drew wet circles with her tongue around each nipple, sucking hard enough to draw a cry of pleasure from Beth who clutched Delia's head to her breasts.

Delia finally stood, drawing Beth into the tent. They lay down together on the sleeping bags, and Delia found Beth's lips again and gathered her into her arms. Beth pulled Delia's T-shirt over her head and then Beth's hands were on her breasts, caressing, kneading, and then her mouth, hot with uncontrolled urgency, was everywhere. Beth seared kisses across her belly and thighs and Delia finally fell back with a low cry as Beth parted her thighs and buried her face in her soft pubic hair.

Responding to Beth's unrestrained passion, Delia reached down and separated the folds of her labia, holding herself apart and crying out as she felt Beth's tongue probe deeply inside her. Later on, at Beth's panted urging, she pushed strong fingers inside Beth and delighted in Beth's orgasms as much as she had her own.

She marveled at the joyous release she experienced in lovemaking with Beth. Unlike other first-time experiences, with Beth there was no hesitation, no fumbled questions about what to do or how. They seemed to know exactly what the other desired and brought each other to the peak of passion as they rushed toward one climax after another.

The sky was beginning to lighten around the mountain peaks above them when their passion was finally spent and they fell asleep in each other's arms.

* * * * *

When Delia awakened, it was late morning; the sun was well above the treetops and Cuzco stood at the edge of the campsite looking towards the tent as if reproaching Delia for having forgotten her. Delia looked down at Beth whose face was hidden by her shining curtain of hair. She tenderly pushed a tendril away from her cheek and leaned down to kiss Beth's face. Beth's eyelids fluttered and then she opened her eyes. She smiled and put her arms around Delia's neck. Pulling Delia down, Beth kissed her deeply.

Once more Delia felt the surge of desire that they had shared in the night flood over them and she allowed herself to be drawn into the kiss.

"It's late," she murmured. Beth's breath was warm in her ear.

"I won't leave until you make love to me again," Beth said, her tongue flicking Delia's ear. "I can't wait the whole day."

Delia crushed Beth to her, the words fanning the smoldering embers that still burned within her. She drew the sleeping bag over them and once again buried her face in Beth's warm breasts, stroking them and kissing the nipples to hear Beth cry out with pleasure.

"Oh, God, I want you so much," Beth whispered hoarsely as Delia's hands stroked down her stomach.

Delia stroked more insistently and she felt Beth's legs fall apart and Delia's fingers found her hot liquid center. The sun filtered through the trees and Delia could feel its warmth on her bare back as she lowered her head between Beth's outspread legs. With languorous motions, she stroked her tongue through the sweetly parted flesh. With each stroke of her tongue, Beth groaned more deeply and with greater abandon. As Delia's tongue quickened, Beth began crying, until she was weeping with joy and passion.

"Oh, please, inside, please," she whimpered and Delia quickly shifted herself and with one swift motion buried her fingers inside Beth. Beth cried out with release and after a few moments pulled Delia up beside her. She held her close, whispering endearments.

When she quieted, Beth held Delia's face between her hands and kissed her, her tongue probing urgently inside Delia's mouth. Delia could feel the wetness growing between her legs, and Beth's kiss inflamed her even more. Her desire for Beth was seemingly unquenchable. As Beth moved between her legs, sliding her belly back and forth against her clitoris, Delia felt fire race along her thighs. The universe contracting to the one incredibly pleasurable thing that Beth was doing to her, she wrapped her legs around Beth's hips and began to rock. Beth rose to her knees and ground her pelvis against Delia's. Delia felt her orgasm begin; soon a cry escaped her lips, and she clung to Beth's hips as pleasure swept her away.

Beth collapsed forward and they held each other, murmuring and stroking each other. Delia felt Beth's fingers trace the appendectomy scar above her groin.

"When did you have your appendix out?"

"My father had my appendix taken out when I was six," Delia told her.

"What do you mean — had it taken out?"

"Before my father took me with him, after I'd

stayed at my grandparents in Arkansas that one year? He took me to the hospital in Little Rock and had my tonsils and my appendix removed."

Beth nodded, understanding. "Because of what happened to your mother?"

"Yes," Delia said. "He stayed with me the whole time, even in the operating room, and watched. Told them he might need to do one on someone some day." She smiled a little sadly. "My father stitched me up lots of times, he set broken bones, pulled teeth —" She stopped. "I learned a lot from him, I'm a pretty good doctor too."

Beth hugged her hard. "Well, you've got a great bedside manner, Doc."

Delia glanced up at Cuzco, who stood just outside their tent, looking at them curiously. "I think she wants her apple," Delia said. "You've spoiled her."

Beth looked at the llama affectionately. "I like to spoil her. She's my baby, aren't you, baby?" Beth asked Cuzco in an uncharacteristically tender voice.

The llama made a humming sound deep in her throat and Delia laughed. "You're the Marlin Perkins here — not me."

After a hurried breakfast of hard rolls, cheese and apples, the two women set off again. A few hours into their walk brought them to a glacier field of gray, dirty snow. At the edge of the snow a featureless pool collected the runoff from the snowmelt. To the left of the snowfield was a steeply rising slope and beyond it a dense stand of trees. As they climbed over boulders and rocks along the outer edges of the snowfield, they could hear the sound of a stream nearby.

They crossed the rocky snowfield, climbed the

steep hill and after Delia checked Jill's map once more, struck off into the forest, steadily climbing. They walked through the trees, their footsteps cushioned by the thick carpet of pine needles, following the sound of rushing water. When they finally reached the top of the slope, they could see the stream at the bottom of a shallow canyon. The women picked their way cautiously to the bottom. Cuzco had no such problems, leaping nimbly from one boulder to the next.

"I wish I could do that," Beth grumbled.

By the time they reached the bottom of the hill, both women's legs were trembling with fatigue and stress. The elevation was taking its toll on Beth, Delia noticed.

Approaching evening brought with it a chill to the air; the shadows grew long and dark. After they had walked downstream for a mile or so, Delia stopped to check her bearings with the compass and the map.

"I think we should stop," she told Beth. "We're too tired from climbing around rocks. We're liable to hurt ourselves if we keep going."

Delia found a relatively level place, hobbled Cuzco and began to set up camp. Based on her observations of Delia the previous two evenings, Beth built a fire ring, gathered wood and had the fire started by the time Delia was finished putting up the tarp.

Delia came over to her and put her arms around her. "I'm going to have to watch it — you'll be taking over my job before long."

Beth nuzzled her back. "Not likely. I'm a sailor at heart."

"Why don't you go get some water?" Delia asked, handing the coffee pot to Beth. "Get the water from a place where the stream is running swiftly."

Delia watched as Beth walked off down the stream with the coffee pot and their canteens in her hands. She turned back to the pot where she was preparing chicken and brown rice and stirred it. She was just beginning to get their plates out of the pack and put them by the fire to warm when she heard Beth cry out.

Chapter Eight

Beth's cry was either alarm or excitement. Delia dropped the lid onto the pot she had been stirring and ran down along the stream until she saw Beth standing with something in her hand. She could see the excitement on Beth's face.

"What is it?" Delia asked. "What's the matter?"

Beth held out the object to Delia wordlessly. Delia took from her a metal canteen covered with olive drab canvas. The canvas was wet and rotted through in some places as if it had been in the water for some time. Delia turned it over and saw written on the back in indelible marker the initials JBD. Delia felt a cold chill, as though someone were watching them, and involuntarily she looked around.

When she realized Beth was looking at her with a puzzled expression, she tried to smile. "Is it Jill's?"

Beth nodded, excitement replacing the alarm on her face. "Those are her initials — Jill Bette Davis." She smiled. "Her Mom loved Bette Davis."

"Where'd you find it?" Delia asked, looking around, unable to shake the uneasy feeling that had now settled in her gut.

"There." Beth pointed to a tree that had toppled over, exposing and trailing some of its root structure in the stream. "It was caught in the roots of that tree. I wouldn't have noticed it except one of our canteens got away from me and floated under the bank down there."

Delia studied the canteen, puzzled over why its discovery made her so uneasy. "Well, this indicates that Jill was here." She turned the canteen over again. "But it doesn't tell us when or where she is now." Delia looked down at the ground. "It's getting too dark now, but in the morning I want to look around here and see if we can find anything else."

"Can't we look now?" Beth asked anxiously.

Delia shook her head and searched the dark shadows among the rocks on the far side of the stream, trying to shake her growing apprehension. "No, it's too dark and besides our dinner is almost ready. I'll look in the morning."

She took Beth's hand and pulled her close. "I know you're excited, but we're both tired and hungry and we might miss something even if we use a flashlight or lantern."

She led Beth back to camp and after they had eaten dinner, sitting in the comforting glow of the campfire, Delia felt her earlier uneasiness fading. Sipping cups of tea, the two women leaned back against the nylon packs and talked about the canteen Beth had found.

"I wonder how she lost it," Beth mused. "Doesn't seem like a good sign, does it? How could she do without a canteen?"

"I don't know," Delia admitted. "We don't have enough evidence to make an intelligent guess."

"You said you wanted to look around the stream more closely tomorrow — what are you looking for?"

"I don't know," Delia repeated. She yawned, fatigue finally replacing her apprehension. "I'd like to get to bed early tonight. I'm really tired."

The lovemaking of the previous night and the stressful trek across the rocks had drained both women; they were content to merely hold each other before falling asleep. Delia could tell that Beth had a thousand questions, but she also knew that Beth realized that she had no answers. Just as Delia was drifting off, Beth whispered, "Dee?"

"Hmm?"

"How long has it been since you had a lover?"

Delia kissed her forehead. "Why? Am I that rusty?"

"Yeah." Beth pinched her arm. "But I think I've got you limbered up now . . . Come on — seriously."

"Five years," Delia said softly.

"Who was she?"

Delia turned over and faced Beth. "It's . . ."

"A long story," Beth finished for her. "I know. But I want to hear it."

"It's really not that long a story," Delia said. "Her name was Robin Sweeny. She was my graduate assistant on a dig in Libya. Robin was . . . I guess like Jill. A hotshot. Hothead. Dramatic. Brilliant." Delia felt the old pain coming back and fought it. "I loved her. I trusted her."

"What happened?"

"She salted the dig."

"I don't know what that means," Beth said.

"Salting a dig means putting fake artifacts in the excavation. We were looking for something specific. Robin was writing a thesis and she had a theory she was too attached to. We started finding particular kinds of artifacts at the top levels that supported her theory. I suspected she was doing it — chose not to acknowledge it. Later on, when it came out, I took responsibility for it." She stopped.

"Is that why they denied you tenure?" Beth asked.

"No. The university never did particularly support my interest in goddess worship, Amazon legends, women's warrior cultures — they always thought I was a little flaky. Said my interests were too narrow — one-sided." She paused again. "But the incident with Robin didn't help."

"I'm sorry," Beth said, holding her tighter. "What happened to her?"

Delia laughed bitterly. "Nothing. The department said it was my fault. I must have encouraged her. They offered me a deal. They wouldn't publicize it if

I'd just leave quietly. Anyway, she got her degree and is now teaching. In fact, she has my old job. Robin is ... ruthless. She'll be chair of the department before long." She kissed the top of Beth's head.

"Don't you ever miss it? Aren't there things you still want to do?"

"Yes, I never found the one thing I wanted to find," Delia said softly.

"What?"

"An artifact that would prove Amazons really existed — that they weren't just a legend dreamed up by a bunch of misogynistic Greeks." She turned to Beth. "I'm kind of obsessive about Amazons. You know how much you liked the stained glass window in my cabin?"

"God, yes. It's gorgeous. Why, is there some significance to the pattern?"

"Well, most people think the half moon represents Half Moon Lake. But the star and crescent moon are also ancient Amazon symbols. According to legend, the Amazons wore boots covered with stars and carried shields shaped like a crescent moon."

"What about the pine tree?" Beth asked.

Delia smiled. "That's my own addition. Because of the mountains."

Beth hugged her. "You'll find an artifact — someday," she assured her. She yawned hugely. "God, I'm fading." She kissed Delia firmly and wrapped her arms around her. "I'm crazy about you, Dee."

"I'm glad," Delia whispered against Beth's face.

Delia pulled the sleeping bag around them and returned Beth's kiss. "You broke down a lot of barriers I'd built up over the years. I should warn you, if you haven't guessed already, after Robin — I still don't trust very easily."

"You remind me of Jill in some ways," Beth told her. "You both love the outdoors — especially Utah."

"Why did Jill come to live out here?" Delia asked.

"We were on our way to California on a vacation," Beth answered softly. "Neither one of us had ever been out West. We'd both lived in Chicago all our lives. But Jill always wanted to see the mountains. She wanted to go through Utah, so we did. When she saw Split Mountain for the first time, it was like she was home. If I hadn't made her go on, I think she would have stayed right then."

"Did she move out here after you two broke up?"

"Yeah, she worked a lot of odd jobs around and then hooked on with the Forest Service." Beth sighed. "We were so different. Jill didn't care about having a career — not like I care. She didn't have the discipline or interest to stick to school or career. She just did whatever job would let her be outside — she was a landscaper, she cleaned pools, she worked in the zoo in Salt Lake. As long as she was outside, she didn't care."

"Sounds like we are a lot alike," Delia said sleepily. "I hope I get to meet her." She was having a hard time staying awake and finally she said apologetically, "I'm sorry but I have to go to sleep."

Beth pulled her over and kissed her. "It's okay. I'm really tired too."

Before they fell asleep Beth asked one final question. "Do you have a good feeling or a bad feeling about finding the canteen?"

Delia considered the uneasy feeling she had of

being watched and then answered with a lie: "I have a good feeling."

They searched the area around the stream thoroughly the next morning. Delia brushed aside pine needles and overturned rocks, once even getting down on her hands and knees.

Finally, she turned to Beth. "I don't think we're going to find anything else. We'd better move on if we want to make any progress at all today."

Beth looked disappointed but helped Delia pack up their belongings.

The path that Jill had mapped out ascended steadily along the rim of a deep gorge that plummeted hundreds of feet to a river that looked like thin brown ribbon. Because of their late start and Beth's blisters which were becoming worse, their progress was torturously slow. They were also hindered by the rugged terrain. After crossing numerous shallow, icy streams, their feet were soaked and cold.

The altitude was also taking its toll on Beth, who was plagued by a ferocious headache only partially relieved by aspirin. As the day wore on, Delia became worried that because they were so tired, one of them might slip and twist an ankle on the rocks. Indeed, they had both slipped a few times, skinning a knee or elbow. When they stopped for a late lunch, Delia consulted the map and saw with relief that the rocky terrain soon ended and they would be hiking through trees again. The map indicated a lower elevation too.

She shared this information with Beth and saw the relief written on her face. The excitement of finding Jill's canteen had worn off, and Delia knew Beth was disappointed that they hadn't found any other trace of her friend during their search.

At three o'clock, Delia called a halt in a thick stand of pines. Beth winced when Delia removed her sock and boot to examine the large blisters which had broken open. After carefully washing the open sores and applying Bandaids to Beth's feet, Delia replaced Beth's wet socks with clean, dry ones, wrapped her in her duster, and instructed her to rest while she set up camp.

As the sun set, a brisk wind swept down the mountainside and Delia noted with some alarm that the sky was filling with gray, wet-looking storm clouds. The temperature continued to drop as they ate a hastily prepared meal, and a heavy dampness settled around them. Delia began to worry that it would snow.

"Sure got cold all of a sudden," Beth said anxiously, looking up at the sky. "It feels like it might snow. What do you think?"

"Yes," Delia said, pulling a wool sweater and nylon anorak over her head. "It could. I wish we weren't camped so close to this gorge. The wind coming up will really chill us." She sipped at the cup of tea Beth had handed her. "I'm going to get Cuzco settled in for the night and feed her. Be right back."

"I can help," Beth struggled to stand. "I'm no wimp, you know."

Delia pushed her back down. "You've proven that already. Just relax."

While Delia fed Cuzco an extra handful of grain and brought her water, she again experienced the uneasy feeling of the previous evening. Since she had spent most of her life outdoors, Delia gave the feeling more credence than she had when they found the canteen. She examined her feeling, wondering if it was the result of her concern about the weather and the fact that she was unfamiliar with the area. But when Cuzco began stamping the ground and rearing back her head, Delia decided not to disregard her instincts which so often over the years had saved her life.

She led Cuzco close to the camp and handed her halter rope to Beth. To Beth's questioning look, she shook her head and put her finger to her lips. Reaching down, she unsheathed the rifle, loaded it, checked the pump action, and knelt beside Beth. The wind was blowing harder now, fanning the fire which leaped up and blew sideways in response to the strong gusts.

Delia felt drops of moisture on her face. "It's probably nothing," she said, covering Beth's hand with her own. "I haven't heard or seen anything — I just have this feeling." She gestured at Cuzco. "She feels it too. I'm going to look around a little."

Beth opened her mouth to protest, but Delia smiled in what she hoped was a comforting manner and stood up. "I'll be right back. I'm not going far."

She exchanged her heavy hiking boots for a pair of moccasins. Donning a pair of ragg wool gloves and a watch cap from a pocket of the anorak, she kissed Beth and set off along the edge of the gorge.

A few hundred yards from camp, Delia skirted some large boulders and a fallen log which extended out over the edge of the cliff. Walking lightly, picking her way quietly along the rim, Delia began to circle their camp. She moved away from the rim of the canyon and crept slowly into a dense stand of timber, stopping frequently to listen and search the rocks below her. She felt comforted by the familiar weight of the 30.30.

As she walked through the growing darkness, snow began to fall and Delia cursed their luck. Snow would slow them down even more. She looked at the ground, searching for any sign of disturbance, any sign that someone had actually been up here watching them, but she found nothing. After she had completed circling the camp, she emerged from the trees to Beth's left and saw with satisfaction that Beth had not heard her approach. Cuzco did however and jerked the lead in Beth's hand.

Beth's head whipped around, and she put her hand on her heart. "Jesus, you scared me," she whispered shrilly.

Delia went over to her. She put her arms around Beth and held her close. Beth pulled away and Delia saw snowflakes on her eyelashes. "Find anything?"

"Nothing," Delia assured her, putting the rifle back into the leather scabbard. "I walked all the way around and didn't see a thing." She shrugged. "It was probably just the wind. Don't worry about it."

"Do you think we're in for a storm?" Beth asked, looking up at the swirling snow.

"I don't know," Delia said. "I want to fix the tarp so we can lower the sides and front if we have to."

Delia busied herself with the tent and tethered Cuzco nearby, not wanting to hobble the llama away from the camp. Even though she had not found any sign of another human or animal, she still felt uneasy. She dug around in the packs and found two waterproof liners for the sleeping bags and made sure the groundcloth was pulled tight.

As they readied themselves for bed, Beth noticed that Delia put the rifle and packs inside the tent beside her sleeping bag. She watched as Delia took out the survival kit and began going through it.

"What are you doing now?"

"I'm checking our survival kit."

"I thought you did that before we left."

"I'm checking it again."

"What's in there?"

"The usual. Matches, a candle, Swiss Army knife, space blanket, leather shoelaces, soup and tea, dried fruit and chocolate, compass, fish line and hooks, extra ammunition for the rifle, a roll of newspaper, nylon rope, plastic sheet, extra socks and sock cap — and the first aid kit."

"You always sleep with the belt pack right by your head, too," Beth observed. "How come?"

"When I'm alone, I sleep with it on. It's a survival pack — it won't do you any good if it's in your other pack."

Beth rested her chin in her hand and looked at Delia. "Could we survive without the stuff in your pack?"

Delia shrugged. "Sure. I've survived some pretty rough situations where I didn't have much gear . . . or medicine."

"Will you tell me about your adventures someday?" Beth asked later when they were snuggled inside their sleeping bags.

"What adventures?" Delia asked.

"Things that happened to you when you were in the field."

"It wasn't that exciting," Delia told her.

"Yes it was," Beth countered. "I know — remember? I read all about you in the magazines. I remember one time reading about how you were attacked by thieves when you were looking for some lost city."

"That was in Tunisia. I was almost killed."

"Well, I'm glad you weren't," Beth whispered, pulling her close. She kissed Delia, her lips warm and insistent.

Later, as they lay together with their arms around each other, Delia heard the wind pick up once again. Her hopes that the snowstorm would abate faded, and she wondered how Beth would react to a suggestion that they turn back. But when she turned to Beth, she had already fallen asleep, and finally, with the sound of the tarp snapping in the wind, Delia too gave in to sleep.

Near dawn, Delia awoke to a sound she thought was the wind snapping the tarp overhead. But as her mind cleared, she realized it wasn't the wind. The wind had died, and she could hear the sound clearly now. She lay still for a few moments, trying to identify it and then sat up slowly. Easing her body forward, she looked outside. In the gray light of dawn she saw the two inches of snow that had fallen while she slept. It was still falling. Something was wrong. A few moments later she realized what it was.

Cuzco was no longer tethered in the clearing.

She looked around and finally spotted the llama about fifty feet away from her. The animal was standing motionless, her head reared back in what Delia knew was an aggressive posture. Puzzled, Delia crawled to the front of the shelter and peered out through the falling snow. Then she saw someone emerge from the rocks above and stealthily approach the llama. At first, because of the long hair gathered into a ponytail, Delia thought the figure was a woman. But as she looked longer, she could tell from his build that it was a man.

Delia's heart began to pound with fear, and an involuntary cry rose in her throat but she choked it back. She hurriedly pulled on her hiking boots and groped behind her for the 30.30. As her hand touched the sleeping bag behind her, two things happened quickly.

Beth woke up and said loudly, "What's going on?"

At that moment, the man with the ponytail raised his arms in the air and shouted at Cuzco who reared up on her hind legs and began running toward the edge of the cliff. By this time, Beth was beside Delia and saw Cuzco heading for the edge.

"Cuzco!" Beth screamed, scrambling out of the tent. Running toward the llama, she seemed unaware of the man who stood motionless watching her and the llama as they both headed toward the cliff.

"Beth!" Delia yelled, groping for the rifle. She finally found it underneath the sleeping bags. She scrambled after Beth. Beth had almost caught up with Cuzco. She looked around and saw that the man was gone. Running blindly through the snow, she went after Beth and Cuzco.

Within an arm's length of Beth, she slipped and fell hard, down on her knees. Off balance, she plunged forward into the snow. The rifle flew out of her hands.

Pushing herself up, Delia looked around wildly — just in time to see Beth make a desperate lunge for the end of Cuzco's rope.

For a moment, Delia thought that Beth had grabbed the rope in time. But the llama was running too fast. The momentum of the animal's flight was too great and she plunged headlong toward the edge. Kneeling in the snow, Delia could do nothing but watch helplessly as Cuzco disappeared over the cliff.

Beth never had a chance. Her hand was caught in the loop at the end of the tether and, though Delia screamed at her to let go, she couldn't. Hands grabbing desperately at Beth's legs, Delia watched as Beth followed Cuzco over the edge. Delia heard the screams of both Beth and the llama as they fell.

Then there was nothing but the silence of the falling snow.

Chapter Nine

Delia lay stunned for a few seconds and then scrambled over to the edge of the gorge. Bracing herself, she leaned over and looked down. An overhang obscured her view and beyond the overhang there was only a swirling gray emptiness of snow. She closed her eyes as despair clutched at her heart. Edging her way out onto the flat surface of the overhang, she looked down as the wind suddenly parted the snow like a curtain. What she saw caused her to cry out in relief and joy.

Beth and Cuzco had landed on a narrow ledge about twenty feet below. It was impossible to determine through the swirling snowflakes whether either of them was moving.

"Beth! Can you hear me?" Delia screamed.

Nothing answered her calls but the sound of the wind and Delia fell silent. She was wasting her breath; she had more important things to do if she was to help Beth.

Suddenly, she remembered the man. Her heart began to thud wildly and she whirled around, searching the trees and rocks behind and above her.

There was no sign of him.

Delia looked around frantically for her rifle. It lay in the snow about twenty feet away. She ran over and picked it up, wiped it free of snow and made sure the barrel was clear. With a quick, practiced gesture, she pumped a shell into the chamber and slung it by the strap over her shoulder.

She calmed herself by remembering the life-threatening situations she had been faced with before. In parts of the world where there was no help to be had from anyone else, she had had to fight for her life. She had been shot at, stabbed, attacked by a shark, mauled by a bear, and in Tunisia a man had tried to drown her. But though she had been frightened at those times, she had never felt the terror that clutched at her heart now. She knew it was because Beth was in danger. Her mind screamed at her to THINK — to DO SOMETHING. But her legs wouldn't move and her brain seemed incapable of telling her body what to do.

Suddenly, over the sound of the wind, she could

hear Cuzco bellowing in pain. The sound galvanized her, and she sprang into action.

She ran back to the tent and pulled a pair of Gore-Tex pants over her sweatpants. Remembering that Beth had gone over the edge with nothing more than her sweatpants and a T-shirt on, Delia donned a flannel shirt and an extra wool sweater over her long-sleeved T-shirt.

Digging through the pack, she found her running shoes and put them on; she would need lightweight, rubber-soled shoes if she had to free-climb up the rock face.

The thought of all the extra first aid supplies inside the large pack was tempting, but Delia decided she didn't want the extra weight on the nylon rope she would be using to go over the edge. She had enough in her survival pack to give Beth immediate care. They couldn't stay on the ledge indefinitely — if they didn't make it, the other first aid supplies wouldn't help them anyway.

She exchanged her wool mittens for a pair of leather gloves to protect her hands from the rope as she rappelled down the rock face. Finally, she took out the yellow nylon rope that she would use to lower herself down the cliff. Pulling its length through her hands, she examined it. It was a new rope, seventy-five feet of it, more than enough to double over and still reach the ledge. Delia could see no frayed places where it might give way. She shook her head. It didn't matter now anyway. It was all she had.

After looking around once more for any sign of the man who might help her, she approached the edge of the cliff. Neither Beth nor Cuzco had moved.

Delia found a stout, firmly-rooted pine tree about five feet from the edge and looped the rope around it, allowing the ends to hang evenly. She put both ropes between her legs and wrapped them around her left thigh. Passing the ropes over her chest, right shoulder and down across her back, she grasped them tightly with her left hand. Then she took hold of the ropes in front of her with her right hand and backed toward the cliff. Taking a deep breath, she short-hopped away from the edge, turning sideways to look down her line of descent, though she could see little through the gray swirling snow.

Cautiously, feeding a little rope over her shoulder, she leaned back, testing the rope. The wind raked her face, making her eyes water. She blinked rapidly to clear her vision and concentrated on moving down the slope.

Brush and small saplings growing out of the rock face clawed at her legs and arms as she rappelled down through the swirling snow. Though she wore gloves, she could feel the heat from the friction of the rope sliding under her hands. The nylon rope was slicker than climbing rope and wet from the snow which was still falling. It was impossible to get a solid grip and her descent was erratic and jerky. The rope cut cruelly across her back and thighs, and she tried not to think of the vast emptiness below and the fact that her life and Beth's life too depended on a rope that wasn't made for rappelling down a mountainside.

Relaxing her grip periodically, slowly sliding down, she tried to keep herself perpendicular to the cliff to keep her feet from dislodging rocks onto

Beth. She spread her feet and went slowly, resisting the impulse to bound down the cliff in two or three long hops.

She tried to banish the fear that made her want to hug the cliff face as she descended. Nevertheless, her stomach contracted with fear when the rope suddenly slipped a few inches and her hands lost their grip. A sudden gust of wind blew her sideways, and she clutched at the rope. Turning her head, she attempted to calculate how much further she had to go until she reached the ledge. Right below her feet she saw that the cliff face curved inward; she hopped back a little to get a better view and found that she had nothing to brace her feet against.

Suddenly, she heard a noise above her and a shower of rocks and snow rained down on her from above. She looked up but the overhang above her head prevented her from seeing the top of the cliff. However, she felt the rope moving back and forth underneath her hands, as if something was rubbing against it.

Or cutting it.

Delia frantically began to play out the rope behind her, sliding as fast as she could, the rope burning a fiery path on the palms of her hands. The rope was new and unless whoever was cutting it had a very sharp knife, she knew she had a few seconds to make it to the ledge. A small outcropping of rocks over the top of the cave provided a toehold and she scrambled to find it.

At that moment the rope gave way, and she found herself slipping down the rocky face.

At the last moment, her feet found the outcropping of rocks below her, and she craned her neck to see how much of a drop she had before reaching the ledge where Cuzco and Beth were. It looked to be about seven feet. Not far, but if she landed wrong, she might break a leg.

Moving her foot cautiously, she found another toehold and steadied herself against the rock face. Slowly, carefully, she bent at the waist and grabbed hold of the rock she stood on. Her fingers firmly wedged into a crack, she eased her legs over the edge of the rock. The ledge was now only five feet below her. She swung away from the rock slightly and dropped to the ledge below.

As she hit the ground, she tucked her body into a ball and tried to roll toward the entrance to the cave. Heart pounding, she lay on her side for a moment. The rope was still in her hands and, pulling it to her now, she could see it had been cut in the middle.

She scrambled into the entrance of the cave and squatted down. Something was moving above her. Seconds later, one of the nylon packs landed near the edge of the ledge, next to Cuzco. The straps broke open as it hit and some of the contents spilled out before it rolled off the cliff. A few seconds later, the second pack sailed past her head, but this time the pack didn't hit the ledge before disappearing from view. The sleeping bags were next, followed by odds and ends that she and Beth had left lying around the camp. Though she longed to try to see who was throwing the equipment over the ledge, she didn't want to expose herself and stayed in the entrance to the cave. She assumed it was the same man who had scared Cuzco into running off the cliff. The same man who had cut the rope. Not that his identity mattered at this point. Whoever he was, his intentions were clear.

He intended for them to die.

She pulled her rifle around and looked up to see if she could spot him. She couldn't.

Although she wanted desperately to get Beth inside the cave, Delia decided it was better not to move for a while. Better to let him think she had been killed. That they were both dead.

So she crouched in the entrance to the cave and looked at Beth. She certainly looked dead. She had not moved since Delia landed on the ledge. Delia's mind raced frantically.

Who was the man and why had he tried to kill her? Was he still up there waiting for her to try to pull Beth inside the cave? Would he try to shoot them? If he wanted to kill them, and he clearly did, then why hadn't he simply shot them in their tent? A thousand questions ran through her mind, but Delia knew she had no way of finding out the answers.

Finally, she decided she could wait no longer. If the man was still waiting on the cliff above them, he might see her and try to kill her again. But if she remained in the cave, Beth would die of hypothermia or her injuries. Besides, she couldn't wait inside forever. She had to get them off the ledge or they would both die.

Clutching her rifle, Delia crept out of the cave and crawled toward the stiff forms on the ledge. She looked up at the cliff but couldn't see anything. Drawing closer to Beth and Cuzco, she could see that the llama's legs were broken at the knees, her thick coat was soaked through with blood. As she crept over to the suffering animal, Cuzco lifted her head and looked up at Delia with eyes glazed with pain.

Beth was sprawled across Cuzco's hindquarters, lying on her back, her hand still looped through the rope. Beth's right wrist was broken; the hand was bent back toward the arm at an impossible angle and the bone, though it hadn't broken the skin, was clearly visible under the skin. In addition, her shoulder joint bulged unnaturally under her T-shirt — dislocated or even broken.

After a quick glance upward again, Delia knelt down beside Beth and checked to make sure she was breathing. She pushed the hair away from her face and exposed a long, deep cut that started near her hairline and terminated under her left cheek. The whole left side of her face was covered in blood, and her left eye was swollen completely shut.

Delia postponed further examination of Beth's injuries until she had her safely inside the cave. She removed the space blanket from the survival kit and managed to roll Beth onto it. She dragged the blanket into the cave which was deep enough to shelter them from the snow and wind.

Delia covered Beth with the space blanket then straightened up, sniffing the air. A faintly rotten smell pervaded the cave — the sweet stench of decay. It was possibly the den of some animal, though how an animal had gotten its prey to this unlikely lair she had no idea. She ignored the smell and walked onto the ledge again. A task awaited her that she dreaded but knew she could put off no longer.

Rifle in hand, she walked back over to her beloved Cuzco and knelt down beside her. She put her face against Cuzco's face and tenderly scratched behind her ears one last time. The llama's struggle had become weaker and she no longer made any noise.

"Goodbye, girl. I'm sorry," she whispered. Then she stood up and fired one shell into the animal's brain. Tears welled up and ran down her face, but Delia turned away. She would cry for her another time. Now she had to try to save Beth's life.

Forty minutes later Delia leaned back on her heels and wiped her sleeve across her forehead. Beth was awake, but her eyes were closed tightly in pain. Delia had crushed up three codeine tablets from her first aid kit and mixed them with a little water which she made Beth drink. Then Delia had set her broken wrist using the roll of newspaper she carried in her survival pack. Delia had also cleaned her battered face as thoroughly as she could with a moist towelette from the first aid kit, closing the deepest part of the cut with butterfly bandages.

Running her hands down Beth's legs assured her that neither one was broken, though one ankle was swollen and bruised. It was impossible to tell whether it was fractured or sprained. All in all, Delia thought, Beth had been incredibly lucky.

A small groan escaped Beth's battered mouth and

Delia leaned down close to her. "My shoulder," Beth groaned. "Hurts so bad."

Delia lifted the space blanket and looked at the grotesquely swollen shoulder. She could see the head of the arm bone clearly through the skin. "It's dislocated."

"Can't you put it back?" Beth was crying; Delia knew that every small movement, even a breath, was an agony. Trying to hoist her up the mountainside in a sling would be unbearably painful.

"Yes. Is the pain still pretty bad? Can you feel the codeine yet?"

Beth started to shrug and screamed. "Hurts so bad."

Delia nodded and smoothed her hair away from her forehead. "Okay. It'll really hurt for a few seconds but then it'll be over."

"Do it," Beth hissed through gritted teeth.

Delia took off her running shoe and sat down facing Beth.

She put the heel of her foot in Beth's armpit. At the first gentle pressure that Delia exerted on the arm, Beth screamed long and loud.

"Okay," Delia said. "Easy now, easy. Just take it easy." On the word "easy" Delia pulled Beth's arm across the center of her body and felt the head of the upper arm bone pop back into the socket. Beth's scream trailed off abruptly and Delia was relieved to see that she had passed out.

Delia removed her foot from Beth's armpit and wiped her forehead with her sleeve. She stood up unsteadily, massaging her bad knee as she straightened up. Delia went outside and looked around for the things that had spilled out of the

127

pack. The snow had stopped, at least temporarily. The sky was still overcast and threatening; it was very cold.

A piece of plastic tarp from one of the packs had blown up against a rock, and she used it to lay the few items on. Most of their belongings — the flashlights, stove, down parkas, boots, food, clothing, all the other medicine in the first aid kit — was gone. Delia knelt beside the small pile of miscellaneous items and shook her head. It wasn't much. Gathering the edges of the plastic together, she carried it back into the shelter of the cave.

This time, the stench of the cave almost overpowered her. Since she had no flashlight and no desire to grope around for the dead animal in the dark, Delia decided to build a small fire. Beth could use some hot tea or soup; she could too, for that matter.

There were only a few sticks on the ledge but Delia gathered enough to build a small fire. Gradually the light and warmth from the fire penetrated the gloom of the cave. Delia cautiously made her way toward the back of the cave where she could just make out a dark, formless lump. Whatever it was was big.

As she slowly approached the form, the stench grew stronger and Delia had to cover her mouth and nose with a bandanna. Her fear returned and with it came a sense of dread and terrible sadness.

It wasn't an animal.

Something glinted in the flames of the campfire, and Delia knelt down to get a closer look. She fought back the impulse to gag on the bile that rose in her throat. She swallowed it back and forced herself to look.

The animals, worms and insects had done their grisly work. The body was badly decomposed. But Delia could clearly make out the name tag on the green uniform jacket of the US Forest Service.

She had found Jill Davis.

Chapter Ten

Trying to avoid touching the body, Delia gingerly removed the gold nameplate from the uniform jacket. She slipped it into the pocket of her anorak and leaned back on her heels. Jill's body was too badly decomposed to examine; not, Delia told herself, that she would have relished such a task. But the discovery of her body raised more questions than it answered. How had she died? And even more puzzling, how had her body gotten into the back of a cave halfway down a mountainside?

Delia backed up and crawled over to Beth who

was sleeping. Looking at her face, drawn and white with pain, Delia wondered whether or not she should tell Beth what she had found.

She shook her head, as if trying to deny the exhaustion that was hitting her like a flurry of blows. The cave was still cold, but the fire had dispelled some of the dank air in the cave. Though the smell of decay was still strong, Delia had no energy to move Jill's body outside. They would have to leave her body here and it would be more likely to be intact if left in the cave. She would decide what to tell Beth after she made some tea.

More than anything, she desperately needed to rest before trying to ascend the cliff. Tiny needles of pain shot through her back and thigh. She knew that unless she rested and ate, she would never have the strength to get herself and Beth up the side of the mountain.

She gathered up the few items she had found on the ledge and put some of them into her survival kit, stashing what didn't fit inside her anorak and pants pockets. The grill she placed over the fire and after filling a small pot with some water from her canteen, put it on the grill to boil. Taking the piece of plastic she found outside, she went to the back of the cave and covered Jill's body, tucking it around the edges of the corpse. When she returned to the front of the cave, the smell seemed to abate and she squatted down by the fire, holding out her hands to warm them.

Beth woke up a short time later and Delia helped her drink some tea. The codeine seemed to be working; when she spoke, her voice was no longer pained.

"What were you doing back there?" she murmured groggily.

Delia sipped her tea, savoring its bitter warmth. On the one hand, she didn't want to upset Beth by telling her about Jill when she was so badly injured; on the other, she knew that Beth needed to know. It was, after all, what she had come here to find out. Dishonesty did not come easily to Delia and she decided to tell Beth the truth as gently as she could.

Taking Beth's hand in hers, Delia stroked the top of her fingers. "I don't know how to tell you this, Beth. I'm sorry but . . . I found Jill's body."

Beth looked at her uncomprehendingly. "Huh? What do you mean?"

"She's dead. Back there in the cave."

Beth shook her head. "No way."

"I'm sorry, Beth."

"Maybe it's not Jill."

Delia reached into her anorak pocket and pulled out the nameplate. She handed it to Beth.

Beth looked at it for a long moment and then turned to look back into the cave. Her face had gone slack from the shock of the news and tears spilled down her cheeks. "Oh, God," she whispered. "Oh, Jill."

Delia wanted to hold her but was afraid to jar her shoulder, so she simply held her hand while she grieved.

"I'm so sorry," Delia said softly, smoothing the hair back from her face.

After a few minutes, Beth looked up at Delia. "What do you think happened to her?"

"I don't know," Delia admitted. "This whole thing — I don't understand."

"Who was that man who scared Cuzco?" Beth asked. "Is she —"

Delia nodded.

"Oh, shit." Beth began crying again. "What's happening to us?"

Delia shook her head. "I don't know. It's possible that Jill fell down here and crawled inside the cave. She may have died of her injuries or —" Delia almost said starved or died of thirst but she didn't want to upset Beth any more. "It's impossible to tell."

"How did *you* get down here?"

Delia realized that Beth had been unconscious during her descent down the cliff and didn't know that the unknown man had cut the rope. She told Beth everything and watched her face work through a range of emotions as she tried to understand the puzzling events.

"But why would he want to kill us? Do you think he killed Jill?"

"Maybe. At first I thought he was just a hunter or hiker who wandered into our camp and accidentally scared Cuzco. But now — it seems like a helluva coincidence. That someone would try to kill us — or at least scare us off — then we find Jill's body. But on the other hand, I guess it's possible. We were following the route she marked on the map." Delia shook her head. "I don't know though. At first, all he did was scare Cuzco — he didn't know Cuzco would run off the cliff or that you'd get pulled over too. I think maybe he just saw an opportunity to get rid of us and took it. But I can't imagine why. It doesn't make any sense. It's like he wanted us to die but didn't want to kill us outright."

"*Are* we going to die?" Beth asked, grimacing with a sudden pain.

"No," Delia said firmly; "Absolutely not. I've got it figured out. First, I'm going to get you into some dry clothes. Then I'm going to make a seat harness for you out of Cuzco's halter. I think you can put your legs through the openings and sit in it — with some alterations. Then I'm going to climb up the cliff and when I get to the top, I'll pull you up."

"You make it sound so simple. Can you do that?" Beth asked. "Are you strong enough?"

"Yes," Delia told her confidently.

"My wrist hurts so fucking bad," Beth said, looking to the back of the cave. She began crying again. "Oh, Jill. God, what happened to you?"

Delia spent the next few minutes getting Beth out of her wet sweatpants and T-shirt and into some of Delia's extra ones that she wore under her clothes. Then, after they each had a cup of soup and finished the tea, she took the two pieces of rope and tied them together in a half hitch knot.

"I'll take this up the cliff with me," she explained, looping the rope through the metal rings on Cuzco's halter. She spread the openings apart. "I think your legs will fit through here."

"Will it be stable enough?" Beth looked at the seat dubiously.

"Sure," Delia said. She helped Beth to her feet. "Can you put any weight on your ankle at all?"

Beth's face was white with pain as she leaned against Delia. She tentatively put some weight on her ankle and her swollen face twisted with pain as she cried out.

"Okay," Delia assured her calmly. "I'll help you get into the harness. Be careful when I'm pulling you up that you don't let your shoulder or ankle get knocked around on the cliff face. Try to keep your back to it."

After both of Beth's legs were in the seat harness Delia helped her lie back down. "How does it feel?"

"It's pretty tight."

Delia nodded. "It has a buckle here, you can loosen it a little." She knelt down and loosened the strap. "How's that? Remember we don't want it too loose."

"That's better," Beth said, closing her eyes. "How are you gong to get me back to the truck? I can't walk."

"Don't worry about that now," Delia said. "One thing at a time. I'm going to pack up now and climb. Okay?"

Beth opened her right eye. Delia could tell that she was exercising every ounce of control to keep from not crying with pain. "What if you fall?"

Delia smiled with a confidence she did not feel. "Then I'll get up and try again. Don't worry. I'm good at this kind of thing. I've climbed a lot harder faces than this one."

She helped Beth outside and gently eased her to the ground. "You just hold onto the rope and try to keep yourself upright and stable when I start to pull." She smiled down at her. "Everything's going to be okay."

Beth reached up with her good arm and pulled Delia down to her in a tight hug. "Be careful."

Delia kissed her hard on the lips and turned away. Looping the rope through her belt, she looked up at the sky. It had stopped snowing earlier, but there was still a blanket of snow on the cliff. Delia studied the cliff, noting potential foot and hand holds. The only real problem was the overhang just below the cliff top. It jutted out away from the cliff, and she knew that since it was the end of the climb, it would be even harder to negotiate since she would be tired.

She reached out for the first handhold in the rock. Arm muscles flexing, she pulled herself up and felt for a foothold. Finding a narrow ledge of rock for her feet, she again searched with her fingers for a crack in the rock and again pulled herself up, fingers and feet working together as she inched her way up the face of the cliff. The rocks under her hands and feet were wet from the snow that had fallen in the night, and once her feet slipped from a tiny ledge and she hung from the rock by her fingers.

Below, she heard Beth cry out, but she concentrated only on finding something for her feet to stand on. After her feet regained their purchase, she stopped and leaned into the cliff, letting her legs take her weight. An icy wind swept down the rock face; Delia felt its cold tendrils freeze-dry the sweat on her face. After a few minutes of deep breathing, she began again.

As she climbed, she wondered what she would find when she reached the top. Would the man be there waiting? Would he try to kill her before she even reached the top? With a great effort, she put such thoughts from her mind and concentrated on breathing deeply. The top seemed miles away and the slippery rocks beneath her hands and feet offered little assurance to her weary legs and tired arm muscles. Her fingers began to cramp from gripping the slippery surface so tightly and her calf muscles burned with fatigue.

Near the top, a shelf of rock collapsed under her hand; she hoped that the rocks wouldn't hit Beth. The stress and exertion of the climb caused sweat to pour down her forehead and into her eyes. As the climb became more difficult, the handholds were less easy to find, and it seemed that every foothold she found disintegrated under the least contact with her feet. The tension and constantly crumbling rocks put her off-balance mentally too and she trembled with exhaustion.

Finally she reached the overhang below the flat rock of the cliff top and rested for a moment on a narrow ledge of rock. Overhangs were the hardest routes of all. Delia leaned against the rock face and forced herself to recall the principles she would need to make it up and over. She looked up at the rock over her head, studying the hand and footholds, planning ahead. It was hard to change hands or feet on an overhang; balance was everything. She checked the rope on her belt that was her lifeline to Beth and reached up.

Keeping both feet on the rock face, she pulled herself up and found a tiny crack for her feet. Remembering to keep both feet on the rock whenever she could, she reached out and found another crack. Climbing quickly, she edged her way up until she was clinging to the underside of the rock. This was the most dangerous part of overhang climbing. One false move, one handhold that wasn't there, one rock that crumbled under her grasp, and she would fall helplessly down the side of the cliff, undoubtedly injuring herself seriously. She pushed these thoughts away, reminding herself that Beth's life depended on her reaching the top safely.

A narrow crack above her head provided a place for her to jam her fingers, and she flung her leg out and hooked her heel into a hole in the overhang. Both her hands were above her head now, her right knee was wedged painfully against the rock face. Her back, buttocks and legs hung freely below her; she could feel the cold wind blowing across her back and legs. Back and arm muscles screamed with the effort of holding her weight, and she dropped her left arm straight down to rest before attempting to make her next move. Pushing her body upward with her feet, she pulled herself up, keeping her feet as close to her body as she could. She bent her legs and raised her body without bending her arms. Again, keeping her feet high, as close to her arms as possible, Delia pressed her feet against a tiny foothold under the rock, relieving the strain on her hands and shoulder. One more lift and she swung her leg up and over and rolled onto the flat rock of the cliff top.

She lay there for a few moments, her chest heaving, the muscles in her arms and legs cramping with fatigue. The rope burns she had suffered on her rappel down the cliff throbbed painfully. Finally she leaned over the edge of the cliff and looked down. She waved to Beth.

"Okay, just give me a few minutes to rest and figure out a way to haul you up." Beth waved back at her and Delia stood up and tied the rope that tethered her to Beth around the pine tree she had used that morning and turned to look at the place where their camp had been the night before.

Everything was gone.

Except for the flattened area where their tarp had stood, there was no sign that a camp had ever been there.

Delia cursed as she realized that whoever had taken their things had taken her canvas duster and her hat. She looked around in vain for anything that he might have left but found only a scrap of plastic from the groundsheet. The sleeping bags, ropes, stakes, their packs, their hiking boots — everything was gone. All they had left were the clothes on their back and the survival kit Delia carried around her waist. There was only enough food for a few meals, and the snow would make hunting difficult. She planned on building a travois when she retrieved Beth from the ledge; pulling it would require plenty of calories. She worried about the man and whether he would return.

It began to spit snow. There was no time to waste thinking about the obstacles she faced in getting Beth off the ledge. She had to act now.

Delia went back over to the edge of the cliff and began peeling the bark away from a section of the pine tree where she had tied the rope. Then, opening the survival kit, she removed the leather thongs and after wrapping the piece of plastic around the peeled tree trunk, she secured it with the leather thongs. At the edge of the cliff she laid another piece of plastic under the rope where it came into contact with the rock edge. Anything she could do to reduce the wear and friction on the rope would increase the chances that it wouldn't break. She then wrapped the rope that was secured to Beth's seat harness around the plastic encased trunk one time. Walking over to the edge she leaned down and shouted to Beth.

"Okay, I'm ready. I'm going to start pulling you up."

Delia pulled on her leather gloves, found a rock behind a tree and, bracing her feet against its base, began to pull on the rope. As she pulled, her arm sockets screaming under the brutal strain, she prayed that the rope would not break and send Beth to certain death on the rocks below. Hand over hand, she pulled the rope toward her, letting the surplus that came up over the cliff coil at her feet. Her arms were already sore from the long climb up the cliff and Beth's weight pulled at her arms, threatening to pull them from the socket. She longed to be able to look over the edge and see how far Beth was from the top.

"When you can, grab hold of the rock and take some strain off the rope," Delia yelled.

She heard Beth yell something in return and became alarmed at the fear in her voice. Delia quickly tied the rope around the tree trunk and ran over to the cliff.

"What?" she yelled down to Beth who was dangling five feet below the edge.

"The rope." Beth pointed to a point above her head. "I think it's fraying above my head."

Delia leaned out over the edge. Sure enough, the rope was pulling apart where she had tied the two ends together. As she watched, the strands began separating, popping under the strain of Beth's weight. Delia stared helplessly down at the rope, her brain screaming frantically. When the last strand popped, she reached out desperately and caught the rope just before Beth began plummeting to the ledge.

The sudden weight of Beth's body pulled Delia violently toward the edge of the cliff and for an instant Delia feared she would be pulled over the edge. Her feet scrabbled in the ground trying to find a foothold. Finally she stopped, a precarious balance attained between her own weight and the dead weight of Beth's body on the other end of the rope.

She looked down directly into Beth's terrified eyes and the desperate look on her face somehow gave Delia the strength to pull the rope. For a moment, Delia didn't think she would be able to pull her another inch toward the top. But as the muscles in her arms and back threatened to separate from the bones, she could feel that she was pulling Beth up.

When Beth was within a few feet of the edge, Delia reached out her hand and offered it to Beth. Feeling Beth's hand clasp her own, she heaved one last time and Beth screamed with pain as her injured shoulder scraped against the rock face. Frantically Delia reached down and grabbed her other arm and pulled on it as well. Beth was screaming in pain. Delia suspected that the strain on her shoulder had probably separated it again but, she thought grimly, it was better than Beth falling to her death. Ignoring Beth's screams, Delia continued to pull her, inch by agonizing inch, over the cliff until she was able to grab Beth's pants and yank her the final few feet over the top.

She lay panting with her head on Beth's back

and after a few minutes she turned Beth over and saw that her shoulder had once again been wrenched from the socket. Beth's face was pale and still.

Quickly, Delia felt for a pulse in her neck and after reassuring herself that Beth was still alive, Delia gave in to her own exhaustion and slid into oblivion.

Chapter Eleven

When Delia awakened, snow was again falling.
Beth lay beside her, still unconscious. Delia knew
that they had to find shelter and stood slowly, her
legs and arms stiff and cramped from climbing the
rock face and hauling Beth up. Her shoulder joints
and arm sockets shrieked in protest as she rotated
them, trying to work out the stiffness. Looking
around, she saw a fallen tree with its root structure
exposed. It would do for a makeshift shelter for Beth
while she built the travois.

Gathering pine boughs, bark and logs, she piled

them all around the massive root system and crawled inside. She opened her survival kit, took out the plastic groundsheet and spread it on the ground. Then she went back to get Beth.

Beth woke up screaming. Delia knew that she would have to put Beth's shoulder back into the socket again, and she knew that this time it would be even more painful. Half dragging, half carrying her, Delia managed to get Beth inside the hastily made shelter. After covering her with the space blanket, she built a small fire near the edge of the shelter and fed it dry twigs. The snow continued to fall as she heated water for tea. Taking two Demerol capsules from her first aid kit, she stirred the powder into the hot tea with a stick until it dissolved.

Then she bent over Beth. "Beth, wake up. I want you to drink this."

Beth rolled her head from side to side and groaned in pain.

Delia put her hand behind Beth's head and helped her sip the tea. "Drink all of it," she insisted. "It's got painkiller in it. I've got to put your shoulder back."

Beth began to cry and the tea ran out the side of her mouth. "Oh, Jesus. Please, not again."

"I know," Delia murmured softly. "But we can't travel with your shoulder out like that. You'd never be able to stand the pain.

"Oh, God, hurts so bad," Beth cried.

"I know. Drink the tea. It'll numb you so you won't feel it as much."

She managed to get most of the hot mixture down Beth. Then, making her as comfortable as she could, Delia pulled off one of her own sweaters to pillow Beth's head. In five minutes Beth had quit crying, and in twenty Delia could see by the blank look on her face that the painkiller was doing its job. The fire was smoking a little from the snow that drifted inside, making her eyes burn.

She studied Beth's face carefully; her color worried Delia. There was no doubt in her mind that Beth was in danger of going into shock. She wished she had the flannel-lined duster to cover her with. She wondered if the man who scared Cuzco off the cliff had taken it.

Once again, Delia set about the task of repositioning Beth's shoulder. She removed her right running shoe and placed her foot in Beth's armpit and she felt the head of the bone slip back into place. A groan escaped Beth's lips, but she was too weak to cry out. Finally, Delia took off her flannel shirt and tore it into strips which she used to bind Beth's arm across her chest.

Finished tending to Beth, Delia turned to her own wounds. She washed the rope burns on her hands carefully with soap and water and bandaged them. Then she leaned back, overcome with weariness and assessed their situation.

She knew they could not go back the way they had come. The terrain was too rugged, and she would never get the travois over the rocks and streams. Beth couldn't walk, and Delia couldn't carry her. They could stay put in the shelter; Delia knew she could snare rabbits, catch some fish, even bring down larger game with the rifle. They would have enough to eat, if the snow let up.

But Beth's injuries needed attention. She might

have a concussion; she could have internal injuries. Delia knew there was one possibility she hadn't considered, didn't want to consider. But now she said it to herself. She could leave Beth and go for help.

Delia rejected the possibility. Beth was too weak and too badly injured. She wouldn't be able to care for herself. It would take two days of continuous walking to get back to the truck — at least. If the weather deteriorated, it might even take longer. By the time she got back, even with a helicopter, Beth might well be dead from exposure.

Delia made herself a cup of tea and took out her maps. She studied them, measuring distances and plotting a course. A thought occurred to her, and she did some quick reckoning. With the tip of her finger, she traced the contour of the cliff they were on. It continued a few miles north and then gradually the elevation lowered as the cliff dropped down into the canyon gorge.

Delia sat back thinking hard. It was their best chance. Probably their only chance.

Beth moaned in her drug-induced sleep and stirred. Her eyelids fluttered and opened. She looked at Delia with an unfocused stare.

"Where?" she said groggily.

"It's okay, we're safe."

Beth licked her lips. "Face hurts. Can't feel my feet."

"Here, let me build up the fire a little."

She added a few twigs to the fire until it again crackled, throwing sparks out into the snow. She moved Beth's feet a little closer to the warmth of the fire. "Is that better?" she asked.

Beth nodded.

Delia tucked the space blanket tighter around Beth's body. "Are you warm enough?"

"Dunno," Beth mumbled. "Can't feel. Am I paralyzed?"

Delia smiled weakly. "No, it's the Demerol. I'm surprised you're even awake and vaguely coherent."

Beth tried to answer her smile. "Pretty tough."

"You certainly are," Delia told her fervently. "I don't know too many people who could survive a fall like that and then be hauled up a mountain." She didn't add — *Especially after finding their ex-lover's corpse in a cave.*

"You okay?" Beth asked.

"Yeah," Delia assured her. "Just tired."

Beth looked around. "Where are we?"

"Inside a tree." She patted Beth's good arm. "Why don't you try to get some sleep? I'm going outside for a little while."

Beth looked panic-stricken. "Don't leave."

"I've got to build a travois to carry you on."

"Can't carry me. Too heavy."

"I'm not going to carry you — I'm going to drag you."

"Where?"

Delia spread the map out. "Well, we can't go back the way we came. It's too rough. I'd never be able to drag the travois without it coming apart."

"In deep shit." Her voice was thick from the drug but she seemed capable of reasoning and Delia was glad; she needed the company.

Delia sighed heavily. "We are. I won't lie to you. It's snowing hard, we don't have much food, we don't have adequate clothes, you need to be in a hospital, and we're three days away from the truck."

"Gonna die?"

"Absolutely not," Delia declared. She pointed to the map. "We're going to hike down to the bottom of the canyon. There's a trail about five miles ahead that leads to the bottom."

"What's at the bottom of the canyon?"

"There's a woman I know who lives in the canyon. I think I can find her cabin. Her name is Wild Rose. She has a snowmobile."

"A hermit?"

Delia smiled. "Sort of. She has a mining claim down there on BLM land. She was an Army nurse in Vietnam. She's quite a character. Doesn't like people very much."

"How d'you know her?"

Delia smiled. "I met her in Robert's feed store one day. She's wild-looking. Dresses in buckskins. She came in one day and bought five hundred pounds of dog food."

"Five hundred?"

"It was her supply for the winter. She has a huge dog, half-wolf. Anyway, we talked about our dogs. She remembered reading about me in an old magazine — said she used it for toilet paper one day in her privy."

"She'll help us?"

"I think so," Delia said. "I'm going outside and build the travois." She patted Beth. "Get some sleep."

Two hours later, her hands stiff with cold, Delia helped Beth onto the travois she had made from two sturdy aspen saplings, the plastic tarp and the remnants of the nylon rope.

Beth was nearly unconscious from the Demerol and stumbled as Delia helped her. After Beth was on the travois, Delia tucked the space blanket around her then put the plastic sack stuffed with their meager belongings in her lap.

"This snow," Beth mumbled. "I'm too heavy."

"It's only about five miles to the trail that leads down to the bottom of the canyon. It's downhill from there. I can do it."

She picked up the ends of the travois, settled the butt ends of the frame into the web belt around her fanny pack, and grasped the saplings in her gloved hands.

The snow was still falling and Delia's running shoes were already wet; under different circumstances, she would have made a pair of snowshoes, but they would be too awkward while she was dragging the travois. She consulted her compass which she had strung on a leather thong around her neck and started off.

Delia had gone less than half a mile when she realized that pulling Beth was considerably harder than she had imagined it would be. Her trips up and down the cliff had exhausted her and pulling Beth up had weakened her even more. As she dragged the awkward, heavy travois over the snowy rocks, she slipped and slid, skinning her shins and elbows. After one mile, it was apparent to her that she didn't have a second wind, and she doubted whether she could even make it the five miles to the trail. Her feet were wet and cold. Beth was probably cold too even though Delia had given her the extra sock cap from the survival kit. But she feared that in her weakened condition Beth would become chilled even more. Once she had stopped and eaten some trail mix and chocolate; Beth had refused to eat anything and when Delia felt her head, she felt hot.

Checking her compass frequently, Delia continued to trudge through the snowstorm. Her shoulders, arms and back, already stiff and aching from the climb, had gone numb from the weight of the travois. She trudged on. Each time she put down the travois and checked on Beth, Delia thought she looked weaker, and her own strength was nearly gone. She longed to stop and find shelter, build a fire, and drink some hot soup. But Beth's weakening condition, and her pale, hot face drove her on.

The ground became treacherously rocky and uneven. Huge fallen trees and enormous boulders that necessitated long detours tired her further. And constantly, one of the long ends bounced over a rock and the travois tipped to one side, threatening to dump Beth out onto the frozen ground.

Long hours later, the silhouettes of the pine trees started to fade into the falling darkness. Delia was beginning to despair of reaching the trail before the next morning when she saw a light through the trees.

Delia tugged on the rope that supported the piece of plastic she had rigged over Beth's head.

"Hang in there," she told Beth. "I'll be back."

Beth's lips were cracked and her face was

pinched and white with fever. "Where ... you going?" she croaked.

Delia had already told her twice, but she knelt down and tenderly smoothed the hair away from her forehead. She was burning up.

"I see a cabin down there — with a light."

"Why are you — leaving me?"

"I just want to check it out before we go down there. I'll be right back."

Beth muttered something and closed her eyes.

Delia stood up. She feared that Beth was bleeding internally. She looked around carefully to get her bearings since she had no flashlight to find her way back to Beth. After studying the trees and rocks around her, Delia set off stealthily through the trees.

As she neared the cabin, she saw that it was larger than she originally thought. It appeared to have two rooms, and on the back of the structure a long porch ran the length of the house. Outside the crudely built structure were numerous fifty gallon drums half-covered by a tarp. An odd smell — sharp and acrid — hung in the frigid air. From the chimney a thin stream of smoke curled, the smell of wood smoke tantalizing Delia with its promise of warmth and light. As she drew closer, Delia saw snowmobile tracks all around the cabin, but though her eyes searched desperately for a snowmobile, she didn't see one.

Something about the scene was disturbing to her; her instincts warned her that something was wrong. Her nerves tingled and a neon sign in her brain flashed DANGER! But what could be dangerous? The cabin was lighted from the inside, obviously someone was in there with a fire. Whoever it was would surely not turn them away.

Nevertheless, remembering the man who had driven Cuzco over the cliff, cut the rope and thrown their packs over the edge, and most of all, remembering Jill's corpse, Delia approached the cabin quietly, looking around nervously for dogs that might give her away.

When she reached the cabin, she crouched down and then slowly raised her head to the level of a window sill and peered inside.

Two large stainless steel pressure cookers sat on a propane stove. In the center of the room were long wooden tables laden with what appeared to be cookie sheets. Inside the cookie sheets was a white crystalline substance that had been baked into thin cakes.

The chill that began to grow inside Delia had little to do with the snow that was melting and running down her back. She craned her neck to look at other parts of the room. On the tables hundreds of Ziploc bags, indelible markers, rubber bands, and other odds and ends littered the surface. In one corner of the room were an old rug and a wood-burning stove. There were weapons too. Pistols, rifles, automatic weapons, and knives. And money — stacks of money, hundreds of thousands of dollars stacked on the tables.

Delia realized she was looking at an illegal drug lab.

She started to back away from the window when

she saw a thin man enter the room from the back. He was tall, dressed in greasy denim and wore his hair in a scraggly ponytail down his back. He was wearing her yellow canvas duster and long-billed cap.

He was the one who had driven Cuzco over the cliff.

He was the one who had cut the rope.

As she crouched outside the window, she realized now why he had tried to scare them away. They had obviously come too close to their operation. And from what Delia could see from outside her window, the man was packing up.

She turned around and slid down the wall to a crouch. Thinking hard, she considered her options. The room was full of weapons, yes, but he was just one person. She might be able to take him out. Normally, she would have backed away and avoided the situation. But she needed the cabin for Beth.

Forcing herself to forget how cold, tired and hungry she was, Delia concentrated.

Then she straightened up and cautiously peered into the window again. What she saw decided her course of action.

There were now three men in the room. All wore automatic weapons over their shoulders and carried knives on their belts. They were talking among themselves as they broke up the contents of the cookie sheets and packed it into plastic bags. She dared not look into the window and so she slouched against the wall of the cabin and strained to hear what they were saying.

"Hey, Snake. When'd he say they'd be here?"

"Coupla hours — three at the most."

"You talk to him or did Charlie?"

"I talked to him, asshole."

"You tell him about them broads and that camel?"

"Yeah, I told him."

"Wonder where they got the camel? Thought only the sand jockeys over in Saudi had camels."

"You think them women found that other broad's body down there?"

"Who cares? They're dead by now. The one got drug over by the camel and the other went down after her. I cut the rope, she's dead too."

"Well, how come we're leavin' then?"

"Think about it, asshole. Three missin' women. Somebody's bound to come lookin' for 'em eventually."

"You shouldna taken the one's coat, Roy."

"Shut up, Charlie."

"You two quit jabberin' and help me get this shit packed up."

Delia crept away from the house, trying not to make any noise as she broke into a trot when she was about fifty yards from the house. She prayed that none of the men went outside and saw her footprints. They would be clear in the fresh snow and if they decided to follow her further, the tracks of the travois would also be clear. She wanted to put as much distance between Beth and herself and the drug dealers as she possibly could.

When she reached Beth, she frantically tore down the plastic and unknotted the rope with frozen fingers. Stuffing both rope and tarp around Beth's body on the travois, she grabbed the poles and began trotting as fast as she could through the trees. The snow was falling harder now, and she hoped her sense of direction was accurate. She felt certain that the trail to the bottom of the canyon was only a mile or two north of where they were now. But with no light to check the map or compass and no stars to get her bearings, she feared she might wander away from the trail.

Beth had not stirred when Delia took down the plastic. It was impossible to see her face in the darkness, but Delia had felt her head and it was still burning up, despite the snow that settled and melted on her face.

Before they found the cabin, Delia had thought nothing could make her go another ten feet. But the knowledge that the men she'd seen had killed Jill and tried to kill her and Beth, the memory of the guns and drugs, the sound of their flat, emotionless voices as they casually discussed their deaths — all this gave Delia a desperate burst of energy. Though her shoes were filled with snow and her feet were numb, she walked as fast as she could, clumsily dragging the travois behind her.

After a half hour had passed with no sign of pursuit, the adrenalin rush left her more exhausted than before. Delia was sure now that she was lost. The snow continued to fall and was so deep that she had to struggle to stay upright. It was all she could do to keep the travois from turning over. Once when she stopped to rest her shoulders and hands, she checked on Beth and grew frantic when she thought she had stopped breathing. She shook Beth which elicited a moan and she leaned back, relieved.

As she trudged on through the ever deepening snow, her feet growing more numb by the minute, she knew that they were both in danger of dying from hypothermia. Her own feet were surely frostbitten, her face and hands were numb, and her legs felt like concrete blocks. She staggered and lurched forward, the travois a hellish weight that she couldn't drop. Concentrating on putting one foot in front of the other, she stumbled on.

Finally, as she was going down a hill, the travois pushing her mercilessly from behind, she stumbled over a rock, pitched forward on her face and rolled. The travois tilted over on its side and as Delia tumbled down the hill, she heard Beth cry out in pain. Snow filled her nose and eyes, and though she knew she should get up, her arms and legs wouldn't obey her brain. In a distant recess of her mind, Delia knew that if she simply lay there, she would die. With one last burst of willpower, she struggled to her knees and began to crawl back up the hill. When she reached the travois, she raised her head wearily.

At first she was confused by the legs blocking her path. She hadn't thought Beth was strong enough to stand. Then as she raised her eyes, she saw that the person blocking her path wasn't Beth.

Beth didn't have a gun.

A surge of rage toward the man who had now surely captured them rushed over her. It wasn't fair, she thought to herself. She had given it her best. After all they had gone through, to fail now. Feebly, she attempted to strike out at the legs with her arm.

Then, with the rifle barrel pressed against her head, exhaustion suddenly overwhelmed her and tears of rage and frustration rolled down her face.

Chapter Twelve

Two hours later, Delia was sipping a cup of scalding coffee laced with bourbon in front of a fireplace. A huge dog with silver-tipped fur lay stretched out at her feet, one of his enormous padded feet resting a few inches from Delia's feet which were now warm inside dry socks.

Their rescuer, Rose Callahan, also known as Wild Rose, leaned over Beth's cot and made a final adjustment to the splint she had placed on Beth's broken wrist, a medical bag open beside her. She had cleaned Beth's face, swabbed it with Phisohex and deftly put ten stitches in Beth's scalp and face. Now she went to a basin of water on a table beside the bed and washed her hands.

"She'll be all right, " Rose said, wiping her hands on a towel.

Delia looked at Beth's face above the blanket that was pulled up to her chin. The black sutures stood out starkly against her pale skin. "What do you thing about her ankle?"

Rose shook her head. "Hard to say. Can't feel any break but it could be fractured. Can't tell without an x-ray."

She walked over to the fireplace and threw two more logs on the fire. The flames leaped up and threw warm shadows across the braided rugs on the floor. Wild Rose's guns, a double barrel Winchester shotgun and a .22 rifle, leaned against the door. A miner's hat hung on a peg by the door and on the table lay big chunks of gray rocks that looked unimpressive but contained gold.

Wild Rose had prospected in the gorge since 1971, building the cabin and woodshed by herself. The mine shaft, located a half mile from her house, had been sunk by adventurous soldiers returning from the First World War and abandoned by them soon after. Rose had reclaimed it from the Bureau of Land Management and had homesteaded the land she lived on near the river for twenty years. The vein of gold inside the mine wasn't wide or deep, but she extracted enough gold to meet her modest needs.

Outside Delia could hear the wind howling down

the canyon walls. "I can't believe we're having a storm like this in September," she murmured to Rose.

Rose didn't answer. She went over to a cast iron wood stove, picked up a battered coffee pot and turned to Delia with a questioning look. Delia nodded gratefully and held up her cup while Rose poured.

Wild Rose was a woman of few words. She spoke only when absolutely necessary, silence flowed around her like a gently flowing stream. She poured herself a cup of coffee and settled into a worn red armchair next to Delia and stared into the fire. Over the rim of her coffee cup, Delia regarded the woman who had saved their lives.

Dressed in black wool pants, a flannel shirt and wide red suspenders, Wild Rose was indeed wild-looking. Her long unruly hair was mostly gray and pulled back away from her face with a leather thong. Her thin face was an impassive map, with deeply etched crowsfeet radiating from the corners of her eyes. If Rose let someone close enough to look into her eyes, they would see the color of the sea on a cloudy day. From her belt, a huge, wickedly curved knife hung in a sheath with the words WILD ROSE handtooled on the leather. Her hands, huge for a woman, were puckered with tiny, star-shaped scars. She wore Army issue combat boots and a red wool watch cap.

Delia thought she was beautiful.

Rose caught Delia looking at her and returned her stare with a questioning look. Delia felt her face redden and shrugged. "Nothing. Just thinking." She motioned to Beth. "You're sure she'll be all right?"

"She needs some x-rays — a cast on her wrist and maybe her ankle. The cut on her head's pretty deep — I gave her some antibiotics. But she'll be okay. Not that much wrong with her."

Delia returned her nod and thought that, compared to the things that Wild Rose Callahan had seen in Vietnam, that was probably true.

After she had met Rose in the feed store two years ago, she had asked Robert while he was milking one night if he knew anything about the wild woman with the huge wolf-dog.

"Middle-aged woman wears suspenders? Has that gold mine up in Ten Mile Canyon?"

"Yes, that's her. She came in today to buy some dog food."

"That's Rose Callahan. She still got that wolf-dog?"

"Yes."

"She was a nurse in Vietnam," Robert said. "Way I heard it the MASH hospital she was in got attacked, blown up. Rose and three other nurses were trapped under the building with some soldiers. She was burned trying to get the soldiers out. Got a Purple Heart and something else."

"Why does she live up there — alone and away from everybody?"

Robert had shrugged, his head pressed up against the side of the cow. "Maybe she saw too much of the world. Doesn't want to see any more."

A solitary person by nature herself, Delia felt a

kinship with the woman who mined for gold and lived by herself with only a huge dog for company. She watched Rose, one scarred hand tangled in the thick fur of her dog, Wolf, the other wrapped around a coffee mug.

"What were you doing out there in the storm?" Delia asked her.

Rose turned to her with a look of amusement. "Might ask you the same."

"It's a long story. You first."

Rose shrugged. "No mystery. I was hunting rabbits. Got caught in the storm. Was on my way home when I saw you come stumbling down the hill."

"I was on my last leg. I'm glad you came along."

Rose said nothing. Finally, "I got a couple rabbits and a grouse. You hungry?"

Delia nodded. "Starving."

Rose sipped her cup. "Soon as I finish this, I'll fix some supper."

While Rose cooked dinner, rabbit stew with carrots and onions, Delia cleaned her rifle and wiped down the barrel. She also sorted through the survival kit and found her extra ammunition. Rose shot her a quizzical look every so often but, typically for Rose, asked no questions. Dressed in a pair of Rose's old wool pants and a fatigue sweater, Delia checked her and Beth's clothes that Rose had hung on a rack behind the wood burning stove.

As they ate dinner — Rose told Delia that Beth needed to sleep more than she needed to eat — Delia explained what had happened to them and also about the three men she had seen inside the log cabin.

To Delia's surprise, Rose nodded. "Yeah, I've seen those assholes a few times."

"You know about them?" Delia asked in astonishment.

Rose eyed her. "Yeah, I know about them."

"And you never —" Delia faltered.

"Never what?" Rose asked, around a mouthful of stew. "Never told them to get out?" She mopped up the gravy with a piece of bread. "I've got nothing against them. Long as they leave me alone, stay away from the mine — I stay out of it."

Delia turned her attention back to her stew. "I'm afraid they may come after us again," Delia said.

"Don't think so. They probably think you're dead."

"Well, what about Jill's body in the cave?"

"Unlikely they'd have killed her, lowered her body off the cliff and then climbed down and put her body in that cave. Too much trouble. They would've just buried her. She probably fell off the cliff, crawled back inside and died of starvation."

"But when I overheard them — they knew about the body."

Rose shrugged. "Maybe they wounded her, she ran, fell off the cliff — they just left her to die."

Delia stood up and took her plate over to the counter. "Maybe." She turned to Rose. "I need to borrow your snowmobile to get help for Beth."

"She's okay for now," Rose said. She looked at Delia critically. "You need to rest before you go anywhere."

"I am pretty tired," Delia admitted. She walked over to the cot where Beth was sleeping. She had some color in her cheeks and seemed better. Looking at her, Delia realized how much she cared about

Beth, how much Beth had changed her life in the short time she had known her. The few nights of lovemaking they had shared had broken down the emotional barriers Delia had erected over the last five years. Beth stirred in her sleep and opened her eyes, as if aware that Delia was looking at her.

"Hey, how're you doing?" Delia whispered.

Beth licked her cracked lips and looked around the cabin. "Where . . . what happened?" she croaked.

"Wild Rose found us," Delia explained.

Overhearing their exchange, Rose came over and checked Beth's arm and the stitches in her head and face.

"Thank you," Beth said.

Rose smiled a rare smile and patted Beth's hand. "No problem." She turned to Delia. "Get some rest. I'll watch out for her."

Delia arranged a pallet of blankets in front of the fireplace and with the sound of the wind whistling around the eaves of the cabin, fell into an exhausted slumber.

When Delia awakened just before dawn, the fire had died to a few glowing embers and a pale light shone through the windows. Rose was asleep in the armchair which she had pulled over next to Beth's cot; Beth was motionless under the wool blanket. The wind had died down and the snow had stopped.

Wolf sat beside the door of the cabin, the hair on his back erect. As Delia watched him curiously, a low, menacing growl came from his throat.

The sound aroused Rose, and she came awake immediately. She glanced at Delia, put her finger across her lips and arose from her chair. Walking across the room on silent feet, Rose picked up the shotgun leaning beside the door and, taking two shotgun shells from a fatigue coat pocket also hanging by the door, slipped them into the gun. Delia lay still while Rose opened the door and slipped outside.

Thirty seconds later she was back inside.

"Get your weapon," she said tersely. "We've got company."

Delia hurriedly pulled on her anorak and a pair of Rose's boots.

"Do you have any binoculars?" Delia asked as she laced up the boots. Rose motioned to a pair hanging on a nail beside the stove.

"Where?" she asked Rose.

Rose pointed halfway up the trail that led to the bottom of the canyon. Moving cautiously to the window, Delia put the binoculars to her eyes. She saw two figures making their way down the path. Both had automatic weapons slung over their shoulders. One of the men was the one with the ponytail who was still wearing Delia's duster and cap.

"Those are the men from the cabin," she said. Delia turned to Rose. "They must have found my tracks in the snow. You should stay here and watch over Beth."

Rose smiled a wintry smile. "I said I had nothing against them as long as they left me alone ... they're not leaving me alone anymore."

Delia began putting the extra ammunition from her survival pack into her pockets and watched as Rose did the same.

"We don't have a chance against automatic weapons," Delia said bleakly. "They'll tear us to pieces."

Rose smiled another of her chilling smiles. "We'll give 'em a run for their money." She turned to the huge dog. "Wolf."

The dog, who had not moved from his position by the door, swung his huge head around to look at Rose with yellow eyes.

"Wolf. Guard."

To Delia's eyes the dog did not change position, but Rose seemed satisfied.

"Is he a good guard dog?" Delia asked.

"No," Rose told her, taking off her red cap and slipping into her fatigue jacket. "He won't bark if someone comes — he'll just attack."

"Okay, how do you want to do this?" Delia asked, looking through the binoculars again. The two men were almost to the bottom of the trail and were separating, one moving to the left toward the woodshed behind the house, the other to the right, toward a rock outcropping beside the river about a hundred yards from the cabin.

"Looks like they're going to circle around," Rose said. "One'll come up behind the house, probably use the woodshed for cover. I'll try and get up above the shed and take him out. The one at the front, he'll try for that rock outcropping beside the river. Just to the right of the cabin when you come outside. You take him. Try and get there before he does." She flicked the safety off the shotgun. "How much ammunition you got?"

"About thirty rounds," Delia replied.

"Okay," Rose said, taking a deep breath. "Let's do it."

Delia looked over at Beth one last time and then both women slipped out the door.

Chapter Thirteen

Delia watched as Rose moved across the porch, then she began to move toward the other end. After the dim light of the cabin, the sunlight reflecting off the freshly fallen snow was blinding. When she reached the end of the porch, she peered around the edge of the cabin to see if she could spot either intruder.

An automatic weapon round chewed a path across one of the roof supports beside her head. She ducked behind the wall of the cabin but not quickly enough. A long sliver of wood from the roof support embedded itself in her cheek. Delia cried out with pain and her hand flew to her face, but she only succeeded in driving the splinter in deeper.

Grimacing in pain, Delia steadied her hand and cautiously felt around until she found the end of the sliver. Gritting her teeth against the pain, she pulled the bloody piece of wood from her cheek. Groping in her pants pocket, she found an old bandanna and pressed it against the wound.

Then she crouched down. She heard another round of fire coming from the other side of the cabin. Within seconds, Delia saw Rose staggering backwards, finally collapsing into a snowdrift at the end of the porch.

Delia ran over to her. Rose was struggling to sit up. She was bleeding from a bullet hole in her thigh, bright red blood splashed across the snow beside her. Delia grabbed Rose as more bullets kicked up little puffs of snow all around them, and they staggered and tumbled back to the porch. Once behind the safety of the cabin, Delia eased Rose to the floor. She risked a look around the edge of the wall and was greeted by another hail of gunfire. By its angle, Delia thought the attacker was behind the woodshed, and she fired off a round in that direction. Then she turned back and knelt down beside Rose.

As Delia cut away the cloth of her Levis with her knife to examine her wound, she might have been looking at a scratch on Rose's finger. Wild

Rose's face was completely devoid of expression. Delia examined the wound; dark red blood oozed up from the jagged hole.

"Missed the bone," Rose said calmly. "Least I think it did. Can't feel anything like a bone nick."

"Did it go through?" Delia asked, trying to match Rose's calm demeanor. As she spoke, she kept her rifle up, ready to fire if the man who had shot Rose appeared.

"Don't know," Rose said, turning her leg over for Delia to examine.

Delia immediately saw the exit wound in the cloth of the pants.

"Yeah, it'll be all right," Delia said, pulling off Rose's belt and tightening it into a tourniquet around her upper thigh.

Rose squinted up at Delia. "What happened to your face?"

Delia wiped at the blood. "Nothing. A wood sliver."

"I think I hit one of them," Rose said. "Watch out for him." She paused, gritting her teeth as Delia pulled the tourniquet tighter to try and stop the steady flow of blood. "They'll move in now," she said matter of factly.

"We've got to get inside and dress that," Delia said. "We can hold them off from inside." Rifle in one hand, she gripped Rose around the shoulders and helped her to her feet.

A scuffling sound at the end of the porch made Delia look up to see a man with his shoulder half-blown off stagger onto the porch. His left arm hung uselessly from his ruined shoulder by a few tendons; great sheets of blood had soaked the front of his clothing. He held his weapon awkwardly under his armpit, but it was raised and poised to fire.

Delia swung her rifle up and shot him once through the chest. The force of the bullet blew him backwards off the porch, and he fell in a bloody heap in the snow.

Pumping another shell into the chamber, Delia ran down to the other end of the porch. She slowly edged half of her body around the corner of the building and caught movement beside the woodpile in the back of the cabin. Dropping down to her knees, holding her rifle upright, she waited until she saw the barrel of a gun come up again and fired off a shot. The chatter of automatic weapon fire exploded above her head, taking fist-sized chunks out of the wood.

When she turned back, she saw that Rose had collapsed onto the floor of the porch. Her face was deathly pale, and Delia knew that she was probably going into shock from blood loss. She had no choice now but to get Rose inside and put a pressure dressing on the wound before she bled to death.

Delia knelt down beside Rose, slid her arm under her shoulders and was again helping her to her feet when she heard a scraping sound from the end of the porch. When she looked up, the pony-tailed man in her duster was standing there, the assault rifle pointed directly to her and Rose.

"Goin' somewhere, ladies?" the man drawled, a smile spreading across his face. He walked over, kicked Rose's shotgun out of the way and reached down to pick up the automatic weapon his partner had dropped in his death throes.

Delia froze, Rose's weight suddenly heavy in her

arms. "My friend is bleeding to death," she said. "I've got to get her inside."

The man continued to smile. "Well, now, ain't that just too bad." He walked toward them slowly, the assault rifle moving around, teasing them. "Put down the rifle and move away from your girlfriend."

Delia obeyed and then stood looking down helplessly at Rose. "She'll die if I don't get her wound dressed now," Delia said firmly. "Just let me get her inside."

"Don't matter," the man said. "She's gonna die anyway." He reached into the pocket of the duster and pulled out another clip which he slammed home into the rifle. "You girls have caused me a lotta trouble," he said. "We had a nice set-up here. Now we gotta move." His voice, playful until now, suddenly turned hard and mean. "I'm lookin' forward to shootin' you — all the mess you made."

Suddenly, Rose stirred beside Delia's leg and reached out with a hand that was covered with blood.

"Don't —" she moaned. "Don't let him — go in there. You know —" Rose's hand plucked at Delia's pant leg. "Don't let him take it."

The man frowned. "What's she talkin' about? What's she got in there?"

Delia shook her head, terrified that the man would actually go in the house and discover Beth helpless in bed. "She's just talking out of her head. She doesn't know what she's saying."

The man swung the rifle butt up and smashed it into Delia's face. The blow caused her to bite down viciously on her tongue and she fell backwards to the floor of the porch, blood gushing from her nose and cheek.

The man stood over her with the gun raised as if to smash her again when Rose yelled.

"Don't hit her, mister," she whimpered. "I'll tell you. I've got gold — lots of it — in a box under the floor. Please. I'll show you." Rose somehow struggled to her feet and started to move painfully toward the door of the cabin, her leg dragging behind her.

The man grinned and moved away from Delia. He reached out, shoved Rose backwards with his arm, and she fell heavily to the floor again.

The man pushed back the canvas duster, revealing an enormous knife. Picking up Delia's gun and slinging it over his shoulder, he turned back to Delia. "You know you ain't bad lookin'. After I get the gold —" He grinned. "We're all gonna have a little party before I blow your heads off."

Delia lay on the floor, her cheek and nose a throbbing mass of pain, and watched as the man wearing her duster put his hand on the doorknob and flung the door open. She knew then that he would kill Beth the way he had killed Jill. The way he would soon kill Rose and her. Helpless rage washed over her.

The next instant a hurtling mass of silver-tipped fury exploded from the door of the cabin as Wolf launched himself onto the man's chest. Delia felt a spray of blood on her face as Wolf's head whipped back and forth, his powerful jaws tearing into the man's chest, arms and finally his throat. Screaming and beating futilely at Wolf, the man fought desperately to throw the dog off, but Wolf's relentless jaws were now firmly locked on his throat. Man and animal rolled off the porch, a snarling, bloody blue.

Delia turned away from the horrible mauling. A few seconds later, it was over.

Chapter Fourteen

Delia sat in the red armchair beside the fire, a glass of Scotch in one hand, a snowball inside a plastic bag in the other, holding it to her throbbing nose and cheek. Her duster, blood soaked and torn, was draped over the back of her chair and her father's cap rested on her knee. She had washed most of the blood from her face, and though her nose felt like it was broken and her cheek was swollen and bruised, she felt lucky. Her rifle, freshly loaded, lay across her knees. Her hands, thighs and back were bleeding where the scabs that had formed had pulled away; her shoulders and legs ached from pulling the travois. Never in her life, she thought, never had she been so thoroughly and totally exhausted.

Rose lay unconscious on a pallet in front of the fireplace, an enormous gauze bandage swathing her upper leg. Wolf rested beside her, his huge head on her arm, his eyes fastened intently on the door.

Although she had lost a great deal of blood, Rose had assured Delia that she would be all right, and after injecting herself with antibiotics, had fallen into a deep sleep.

Delia rose stiffly from her chair, wincing at the pain, and crossed the room to Beth's cot. She picked up Beth's hand and waited until she opened her eyes.

"What's going on?" Beth asked drowsily. "What was all that noise I heard?" She squinted up at Delia, who still had the icepack against her face. "What the hell happened to you?"

"Nothing," Delia mumbled around her swollen jaw. "Everything's okay now." She sat down wearily on the edge of the bed. "I'll tell you all about it later. Sleep now."

Beth shook her head. "I'm not tired anymore. What happened to your face?"

"My damn nose is broken."

Beth raised an eyebrow and winced as the facial movement tightened her stitches. "There's no need to curse," she teased. "Why don't you put that gun way and lie down here beside me?" Beth inched over to make room for Delia on the cot.

Delia stretched out beside Beth, her back against the footboard, and put the rifle down beside her.

"Does it hurt much?" Beth asked.

"Yeah," Delia admitted, her voice muffled by the ice bag. "It hurts a lot. Everything hurts."

Beth raised her head up a little and rearranged her pillow so she could look at Delia. "What happened out there?" She looked over at Rose who was still sleeping. "Is she going to be all right?"

Delia nodded. "I think so." She sighed wearily. "As soon as I get some rest and the swelling goes down a little I'll take Rose's snowmobile and get some help. You two have to be airlifted out. But I need a couple of days to get my strength back." She moved the icebag away from her face, revealing her broken nose and cheek to Beth.

"Oh, my God, Dee," Beth gasped. "You look terrible. Do you think it's broken?"

"I know my nose is broken," Delia said. "I'm not sure about the cheek, but I don't think I could talk this good if my jaw was broken. It looks bad now because it just happened. In a couple of days I'll just have a black eye."

"What about those men?" Beth asked, her voice fearful.

Delia gave her a brief summary of the confrontation.

"What about the third man in the cabin? What happened to him?"

"I assume he took off with the drugs and money; I doubt he'll come back, but I'm not taking any chances." She patted the rifle beside her on the bed.

"What do you think happened to Jill? Do you think she was ... you know, mixed up with those people?"

"No," Delia assured her. "But unless they catch

177

the guy who got away I don't think we'll ever know for sure. My guess is Jill ran across the drug lab when she was doing her job and, from what you told me about her, I don't think she told anyone at the Forest Service about it. She wanted to get proof first — she wanted to get total credit for finding these guys. So maybe she waited for the weekend, got her binoculars and camera and went back to take pictures. But something went wrong and they killed her."

"But how did she get in that cave?"

"I don't know," Delia admitted.

"Don't you think it's a coincidence that we went over the same cliff?"

"Not really," Delia said. "I mean we were following the map that Jill marked out — I think what happened to her is probably what happened to us. It could have happened so many ways. But I don't think she was dead when she went over the cliff. There's no way she could have gotten that far back in the cave if she hadn't crawled."

"Do you think . . . they threw her off?"

"Maybe," Delia said softly. "Or maybe she was wounded somehow and went over the edge in the dark — or she might have tried to climb down to get away from them and hurt herself so badly she couldn't get back up again." Delia sighed. "They'll be able to tell us more after they recover the body and do an autopsy."

Beth started to cry softly and Delia scooted up on the bed to hold her.

"Oh, Jill," Beth whispered. "She died by herself back there — alone and in the dark."

Delia patted Beth's back while she grieved for

178

her friend. Delia suddenly felt weariness wash over her like a wave. She released Beth and fell back against the pillows.

"You're exhausted," Beth mumbled, wiping her eyes. "I'm sorry. You must be in terrible pain."

"We're both a mess," Delia said. "Look at us."

"What's going to happen to us?" Beth asked.

"I told you," Delia said. "In a couple of days I'll go out and —"

"Not that, silly. I mean — the future."

"I don't know. What do you want to happen?"

"I want to be with you," Beth said simply.

Delia slipped her arms around Beth and gently kissed her cheek. "I want the same. But I should warn you — I'm not very good about trusting people. And I don't like the city. I could never live in Chicago." She looked up at Beth, wincing at the pain in her nose and jaw. "Could you get used to living in the wilderness — without a telephone?"

"A few weeks ago I wouldn't have been able to imagine going one day without my phone," Beth said sleepily. "I dunno. I might have to go back to Chicago once in a while for a real hotdog or deep-dish pizza."

"I think I could let you go for that long," Delia murmured.

"Why don't you try and get some sleep? Let me watch over you for a change?" Beth suggested.

"Okay, it's a deal," Delia said. She turned to look at Wolf.

"Wolf," Delia said.

The big dog raised his head and looked at her intently.

"Wolf — guard."

Beth looked at Delia with a puzzled expression. "Will he bark if someone tries to come in?"

Delia smiled and closed her eyes. "No, but believe me — we're safe."

A few of the publications of
THE NAIAD PRESS, INC.
P.O. Box 10543 • Tallahassee, Florida 32302
Phone (904) 539-5965
Mail orders welcome. Please include 15% postage.

STICKS AND STONES by Jackie Calhoun. 208 pp. Contemporary
lesbian lives and loves.   ISBN 1-56280-020-5 $9.95

DELIA IRONFOOT by Jeane Harris. 192 pp. Adventure for Delia
and Beth in the Utah mountains.   ISBN 1-56280-014-0   9.95

UNDER THE SOUTHERN CROSS by Claire McNab. 192 pp.
Romantic nights Down Under.   ISBN 1-56280-011-6   9.95

RIVERFINGER WOMEN by Elana Nachman/Dykewomon.
208 pp. Classic Lesbian/feminist novel.   ISBN 1-56280-013-2   8.95

A CERTAIN DISCONTENT by Cleve Boutell. 240 pp. A unique
coterie of women.   ISBN 1-56280-009-4   9.95

GRASSY FLATS by Penny Hayes. 256 pp. Lesbian romance in
the '30s.   ISBN 1-56280-010-8   9.95

A SINGULAR SPY by Amanda K. Williams. 192 pp. 3rd spy novel
featuring Lesbian agent Madison McGuire.   ISBN 1-56280-008-6   8.95

THE END OF APRIL by Penny Sumner. 240 pp. A Victoria Cross
Mystery. First in a series.   ISBN 1-56280-007-8   8.95

A FLIGHT OF ANGELS by Sarah Aldridge. 240 pp. Romance set at
the National Gallery of Art   ISBN 1-56280-001-9   9.95

HOUSTON TOWN by Deborah Powell. 208 pp. A Hollis Carpenter
mystery. Second in a series.   ISBN 1-56280-006-X   8.95

KISS AND TELL by Robbi Sommers. 192 pp. Scorching stories by
the author of *Pleasures*.   ISBN 1-56280-005-1   8.95

STILL WATERS by Pat Welch. 208 pp. Second in the Helen
Black mystery series.   ISBN 0-941483-97-5   8.95

MURDER IS GERMANE by Karen Saum. 224 pp. The 2nd
Brigid Donovan mystery.   ISBN 0-941483-98-3   8.95

TO LOVE AGAIN by Evelyn Kennedy. 208 pp. Wildly
romantic love story.   ISBN 0-941483-85-1   9.95

IN THE GAME by Nikki Baker. 192 pp. A Virginia Kelly
mystery. First in a series.   ISBN 01-56280-004-3   8.95

AVALON by Mary Jane Jones. 256 pp. A Lesbian Arthurian
romance.   ISBN 0-941483-96-7   9.95

STRANDED by Camarin Grae. 320 pp. Entertaining, riveting
adventure.   ISBN 0-941483-99-1   9.95

THE DAUGHTERS OF ARTEMIS by Lauren Wright Douglas.
240 pp. Third Caitlin Reece mystery. ISBN 0-941483-95-9   8.95

CLEARWATER by Catherine Ennis. 176 pp. Romantic secrets
of a small Louisiana town. ISBN 0-941483-65-7   8.95

THE HALLELUJAH MURDERS by Dorothy Tell. 176 pp.
Second Poppy Dillworth mystery. ISBN 0-941483-88-6   8.95

ZETA BASE by Judith Alguire. 208 pp. Lesbian triangle
on a future Earth. ISBN 0-941483-94-0   9.95

SECOND CHANCE by Jackie Calhoun. 256 pp. Contemporary
Lesbian lives and loves. ISBN 0-941483-93-2   9.95

MURDER BY TRADITION by Katherine V. Forrest. 288 pp.
A Kate Delafield Mystery. 4th in a series. ISBN 0-941483-89-4   18.95

BENEDICTION by Diane Salvatore. 272 pp. Striking,
contemporary romantic novel. ISBN 0-941483-90-8   9.95

CALLING RAIN by Karen Marie Christa Minns. 240 pp.
Spellbinding, erotic love story ISBN 0-941483-87-8   9.95

BLACK IRIS by Jeane Harris. 192 pp. Caroline's hidden past . . .
ISBN 0-941483-68-1   8.95

TOUCHWOOD by Karin Kallmaker. 240 pp. Loving, May/
December romance. ISBN 0-941483-76-2   8.95

BAYOU CITY SECRETS by Deborah Powell. 224 pp. A Hollis
Carpenter mystery. First in a series. ISBN 0-941483-91-6   8.95

COP OUT by Claire McNab. 208 pp. 4th Det. Insp. Carol Ashton
mystery. ISBN 0-941483-84-3   8.95

LODESTAR by Phyllis Horn. 224 pp. Romantic, fast-moving
adventure. ISBN 0-941483-83-5   8.95

THE BEVERLY MALIBU by Katherine V. Forrest. 288 pp. A
Kate Delafield Mystery. 3rd in a series. (HC) ISBN 0-941483-47-9   16.95
Paperback ISBN 0-941483-48-7   9.95

THAT OLD STUDEBAKER by Lee Lynch. 272 pp. Andy's affair
with Regina and her attachment to her beloved car.
ISBN 0-941483-82-7   9.95

PASSION'S LEGACY by Lori Paige. 224 pp. Sarah is swept into
the arms of Augusta Pym in this delightful historical romance.
ISBN 0-941483-81-9   8.95

THE PROVIDENCE FILE by Amanda Kyle Williams. 256 pp.
Second espionage thriller featuring lesbian agent Madison McGuire
ISBN 0-941483-92-4   8.95

I LEFT MY HEART by Jaye Maiman. 320 pp. A Robin Miller
Mystery. First in a series. ISBN 0-941483-72-X   9.95

THE PRICE OF SALT by Patricia Highsmith (writing as Claire
Morgan). 288 pp. Classic lesbian novel, first issued in 1952 . . .

acknowledged by its author under her own, very famous, name.
ISBN 1-56280-003-5   8.95

SIDE BY SIDE by Isabel Miller. 256 pp. From beloved author of
Patience and Sarah.   ISBN 0-941483-77-0   8.95

SOUTHBOUND by Sheila Ortiz Taylor. 240 pp. Hilarious sequel
to *Faultline.*   ISBN 0-941483-78-9   8.95

STAYING POWER: LONG TERM LESBIAN COUPLES
by Susan E. Johnson. 352 pp. Joys of coupledom.
ISBN 0-941-483-75-4   12.95

SLICK by Camarin Grae. 304 pp. Exotic, erotic adventure.
ISBN 0-941483-74-6   9.95

NINTH LIFE by Lauren Wright Douglas. 256 pp. A Caitlin
Reece mystery. 2nd in a series.   ISBN 0-941483-50-9   8.95

PLAYERS by Robbi Sommers. 192 pp. Sizzling, erotic novel.
ISBN 0-941483-73-8   8.95

MURDER AT RED ROOK RANCH by Dorothy Tell. 224 pp.
First Poppy Dillworth adventure.   ISBN 0-941483-80-0   8.95

LESBIAN SURVIVAL MANUAL by Rhonda Dicksion.
112 pp. Cartoons!   ISBN 0-941483-71-1   8.95

A ROOM FULL OF WOMEN by Elisabeth Nonas. 256 pp.
Contemporary Lesbian lives.   ISBN 0-941483-69-X   8.95

MURDER IS RELATIVE by Karen Saum. 256 pp. The first
Brigid Donovan mystery.   ISBN 0-941483-70-3   8.95

PRIORITIES by Lynda Lyons 288 pp. Science fiction with
a twist.   ISBN 0-941483-66-5   8.95

THEME FOR DIVERSE INSTRUMENTS by Jane Rule. 208
pp. Powerful romantic lesbian stories.   ISBN 0-941483-63-0   8.95

LESBIAN QUERIES by Hertz & Ertman. 112 pp. The questions
you were too embarrassed to ask.   ISBN 0-941483-67-3   8.95

CLUB 12 by Amanda Kyle Williams. 288 pp. Espionage thriller
featuring a lesbian agent!   ISBN 0-941483-64-9   8.95

DEATH DOWN UNDER by Claire McNab. 240 pp. 3rd Det.
Insp. Carol Ashton mystery.   ISBN 0-941483-39-8   8.95

MONTANA FEATHERS by Penny Hayes. 256 pp. Vivian and
Elizabeth find love in frontier Montana.   ISBN 0-941483-61-4   8.95

CHESAPEAKE PROJECT by Phyllis Horn. 304 pp. Jessie &
Meredith in perilous adventure.   ISBN 0-941483-58-4   8.95

LIFESTYLES by Jackie Calhoun. 224 pp. Contemporary Lesbian
lives and loves.   ISBN 0-941483-57-6   8.95

VIRAGO by Karen Marie Christa Minns. 208 pp. Darsen has
chosen Ginny.   ISBN 0-941483-56-8   8.95

WILDERNESS TREK by Dorothy Tell. 192 pp. Six women on
vacation learning "new" skills.   ISBN 0-941483-60-6   8.95

MURDER BY THE BOOK by Pat Welch. 256 pp. A Helen
Black Mystery. First in a series.   ISBN 0-941483-59-2   8.95

BERRIGAN by Vicki P. McConnell. 176 pp. Youthful Lesbian —
romantic, idealistic Berrigan.   ISBN 0-941483-55-X   8.95

LESBIANS IN GERMANY by Lillian Faderman & B. Eriksson.
128 pp. Fiction, poetry, essays.   ISBN 0-941483-62-2   8.95

THERE'S SOMETHING I'VE BEEN MEANING TO TELL
YOU Ed. by Loralee MacPike. 288 pp. Gay men and lesbians
coming out to their children.   ISBN 0-941483-44-4   9.95
                                               ISBN 0-941483-54-1   16.95

LIFTING BELLY by Gertrude Stein. Ed. by Rebecca Mark. 104
pp. Erotic poetry.   ISBN 0-941483-51-7   8.95
                                               ISBN 0-941483-53-3   14.95

ROSE PENSKI by Roz Perry. 192 pp. Adult lovers in a long-term
relationship.   ISBN 0-941483-37-1   8.95

AFTER THE FIRE by Jane Rule. 256 pp. Warm, human novel
by this incomparable author.   ISBN 0-941483-45-2   8.95

SUE SLATE, PRIVATE EYE by Lee Lynch. 176 pp. The gay
folk of Peacock Alley are *all cats*.   ISBN 0-941483-52-5   8.95

CHRIS by Randy Salem. 224 pp. Golden oldie. Handsome Chris
and her adventures.   ISBN 0-941483-42-8   8.95

THREE WOMEN by March Hastings. 232 pp. Golden oldie. A
triangle among wealthy sophisticates.   ISBN 0-941483-43-6   8.95

RICE AND BEANS by Valeria Taylor. 232 pp. Love and
romance on poverty row.   ISBN 0-941483-41-X   8.95

PLEASURES by Robbi Sommers. 204 pp. Unprecedented
eroticism.   ISBN 0-941483-49-5   8.95

EDGEWISE by Camarin Grae. 372 pp. Spellbinding
adventure.   ISBN 0-941483-19-3   9.95

FATAL REUNION by Claire McNab. 224 pp. 2nd Det. Inspec.
Carol Ashton mystery.   ISBN 0-941483-40-1   8.95

KEEP TO ME STRANGER by Sarah Aldridge. 372 pp. Romance
set in a department store dynasty.   ISBN 0-941483-38-X   9.95

HEARTSCAPE by Sue Gambill. 204 pp. American lesbian in
Portugal.   ISBN 0-941483-33-9   8.95

IN THE BLOOD by Lauren Wright Douglas. 252 pp. Lesbian
science fiction adventure fantasy   ISBN 0-941483-22-3   8.95

THE BEE'S KISS by Shirley Verel. 216 pp. Delicate, delicious
romance.   ISBN 0-941483-36-3   8.95

RAGING MOTHER MOUNTAIN by Pat Emmerson. 264 pp.
Furosa Firechild's adventures in Wonderland.   ISBN 0-941483-35-5   8.95

IN EVERY PORT by Karin Kallmaker. 228 pp. Jessica's sexy,
adventuresome travels.   ISBN 0-941483-37-7   8.95

OF LOVE AND GLORY by Evelyn Kennedy. 192 pp. Exciting
WWII romance.   ISBN 0-941483-32-0   8.95

CLICKING STONES by Nancy Tyler Glenn. 288 pp. Love
transcending time.   ISBN 0-941483-31-2   9.95

SURVIVING SISTERS by Gail Pass. 252 pp. Powerful love
story.   ISBN 0-941483-16-9   8.95

SOUTH OF THE LINE by Catherine Ennis. 216 pp. Civil War
adventure.   ISBN 0-941483-29-0   8.95

WOMAN PLUS WOMAN by Dolores Klaich. 300 pp. Supurb
Lesbian overview.   ISBN 0-941483-28-2   9.95

SLOW DANCING AT MISS POLLY'S by Sheila Ortiz Taylor.
96 pp. Lesbian Poetry   ISBN 0-941483-30-4   7.95

DOUBLE DAUGHTER by Vicki P. McConnell. 216 pp. A Nyla
Wade Mystery, third in the series.   ISBN 0-941483-26-6   8.95

HEAVY GILT by Delores Klaich. 192 pp. Lesbian detective/
disappearing homophobes/upper class gay society.

                                              ISBN 0-941483-25-8   8.95

THE FINER GRAIN by Denise Ohio. 216 pp. Brilliant young
college lesbian novel.   ISBN 0-941483-11-8   8.95

THE AMAZON TRAIL by Lee Lynch. 216 pp. Life, travel & lore
of famous lesbian author.   ISBN 0-941483-27-4   8.95

HIGH CONTRAST by Jessie Lattimore. 264 pp. Women of the
Crystal Palace.   ISBN 0-941483-17-7   8.95

OCTOBER OBSESSION by Meredith More. Josie's rich, secret
Lesbian life.   ISBN 0-941483-18-5   8.95

LESBIAN CROSSROADS by Ruth Baetz. 276 pp. Contemporary
Lesbian lives.   ISBN 0-941483-21-5   9.95

BEFORE STONEWALL: THE MAKING OF A GAY AND
LESBIAN COMMUNITY by Andrea Weiss & Greta Schiller.
96 pp., 25 illus.   ISBN 0-941483-20-7   7.95

WE WALK THE BACK OF THE TIGER by Patricia A. Murphy.
192 pp. Romantic Lesbian novel/beginning women's movement.
                                              ISBN 0-941483-13-4   8.95

SUNDAY'S CHILD by Joyce Bright. 216 pp. Lesbian athletics, at
last the novel about sports.   ISBN 0-941483-12-6   8.95

OSTEN'S BAY by Zenobia N. Vole. 204 pp. Sizzling adventure
romance set on Bonaire.   ISBN 0-941483-15-0   8.95

LESSONS IN MURDER by Claire McNab. 216 pp. 1st Det. Inspec.
Carol Ashton mystery — erotic tension!. ISBN 0-941483-14-2   8.95

YELLOWTHROAT by Penny Hayes. 240 pp. Margarita, bandit,
kidnaps Julia. ISBN 0-941483-10-X   8.95

SAPPHISTRY: THE BOOK OF LESBIAN SEXUALITY by
Pat Califia. 3d edition, revised. 208 pp. ISBN 0-941483-24-X   8.95

CHERISHED LOVE by Evelyn Kennedy. 192 pp. Erotic
Lesbian love story. ISBN 0-941483-08-8   8.95

LAST SEPTEMBER by Helen R. Hull. 208 pp. Six stories & a
glorious novella. ISBN 0-941483-09-6   8.95

THE SECRET IN THE BIRD by Camarin Grae. 312 pp. Striking,
psychological suspense novel. ISBN 0-941483-05-3   8.95

TO THE LIGHTNING by Catherine Ennis. 208 pp. Romantic
Lesbian 'Robinson Crusoe' adventure. ISBN 0-941483-06-1   8.95

THE OTHER SIDE OF VENUS by Shirley Verel. 224 pp.
Luminous, romantic love story. ISBN 0-941483-07-X   8.95

DREAMS AND SWORDS by Katherine V. Forrest. 192 pp.
Romantic, erotic, imaginative stories. ISBN 0-941483-03-7   8.95

MEMORY BOARD by Jane Rule. 336 pp. Memorable novel
about an aging Lesbian couple. ISBN 0-941483-02-9   9.95

THE ALWAYS ANONYMOUS BEAST by Lauren Wright
Douglas. 224 pp. A Caitlin Reece mystery. First in a series.
ISBN 0-941483-04-5   8.95

SEARCHING FOR SPRING by Patricia A. Murphy. 224 pp.
Novel about the recovery of love. ISBN 0-941483-00-2   8.95

DUSTY'S QUEEN OF HEARTS DINER by Lee Lynch. 240 pp.
Romantic blue-collar novel. ISBN 0-941483-01-0   8.95

PARENTS MATTER by Ann Muller. 240 pp. Parents'
relationships with Lesbian daughters and gay sons.
ISBN 0-930044-91-6   9.95

THE PEARLS by Shelley Smith. 176 pp. Passion and fun in
the Caribbean sun. ISBN 0-930044-93-2   7.95

MAGDALENA by Sarah Aldridge. 352 pp. Epic Lesbian novel
set on three continents. ISBN 0-930044-99-1   8.95

These are just a few of the many Naiad Press titles — we are the oldest and
largest lesbian/feminist publishing company in the world. Please request a
complete catalog. We offer personal service; we encourage and welcome direct
mail orders from individuals who have limited access to bookstores carrying
our publications.